DOC HOLLIDAY

THE HARD RIDE

DAVID TIENTER

DOC HOLLIDAY: THE HARD RIDE
by
David Tienter

Copyright © David Tienter 2014
Edited by: Joann Smith
Cover Illustration Copyright © 2014 by Ravenswood
Publishing
Published by Enigma Press
(An Imprint of Ravenswood Publishing)

GMTA Publishing Group, LLC
6296 Philippi Church Rd.
Raeford, NC 28376
http://www.gmtapublishing.com

Printed in the U.S.A.

ISBN-13: 978-0692326633
ISBN-10: 0692326634

DEDICATION

I lovingly dedicate this work to my three sisters, Peg, Chris, and Jinny. No one can ever have too many sisters. We all need their support.

TABLE OF CONTENTS

DAVID TIENTER

CHAPTER ONE

"Please hurry that coffee along would you, Rosie, my dear? Kate and I seem to find ourselves overly thirsty for your delightful elixir this morning." Tom was dressed in a light brown suit and derby, an unusual sight here on the dusty sun-baked streets of Jackboro, Texas. The usual wear was either cowboys sweat caked denim or soldiers blue uniforms. Kate, his companion, wore a simple yellow dress tied behind her in a large bow. Her hair was covered by a flowered bonnet. Her mood was much fouler than his as she had consumed large quantities of cheap whiskey and been busy until late in the night. She had not had the usual eye-opener before coming down to eat.

Dr. Tom McKay had stayed late at his poker game. The glass of 'cough medicine' he drank upon awakening helped mellow out his mood.

"John, are you having food this morning, or are you just getting your nourishment from that cigarette and cough medicine?"

"Kate, my dear, please do not call me John. My name, for now, must remain Tom. Remember that nasty little warrant for the arrest of John Holliday is still current back in the hell known as East Texas. However, in answer to your query, I find myself a bit peckish, Love. Eggs Benedict and venison steak for me please."

Kate crossed the room and gave Tom's order to Rosie. A loud laugh and subsequent burst of coughing ensued. Rosie cooked steak and eggs for breakfast. If she was feeling extremely generous and had them close at hand, she might toss a hard biscuit on the plate, but there was no chance for anything else in Rosie's establishment. This was not an eatery with waitresses that wrote down orders or ciphered your check. Forty cents for breakfast. Take what you get, don't mouth back too much to Rosie and you may be welcomed back.

God dammit Tom," said Rosie, coming to the door to look at him while she wiped her hands and face with what had once been a clean white towel. "Eggs Benedict and venison steak. Shit, you start me laughing back there and then I start coughing. Just makes me get further behind back here. I do like that order though. I'm going to write it down and someday I might even have it for you, if I ever figure out how to make it. What time you setting up over in the meadow?

Cal's got a tooth bothering him and I will probably send him over to see you."

"I'm heading on over as soon as I battle my way through the eggs and gristle you have embellished my plate with. You should feel proud I love you so much. Otherwise I'd entertain the notion to shoot you just to get a new cook back there."

Tom, a regular diner here, had agreed to provide dental services this morning for the 'Jackboro Celebration'. The mayor had not said what the celebration was for when he approached Tom, who was one of the few licensed dentists in Texas. He seldom practiced that profession. He ran the faro table and a poker game at Dega's bar. The mayor had dropped over a hundred at the poker table, right before he asked and Tom had been feeling generous.

He deeply regretted it now. Five hours in West Texas sunshine pulling teeth would not be enjoyable. He felt his morning would be better spent returning to the hotel and helping Kate remove that bright yellow dress she was wearing. It was early in the morning for her, she was hung over, her eyes bloodshot, her breath almost caustic, still she was a beauty, and close at hand.

Maybe he could finish early before she went to the bar. Being the best looking whore in the state, once she was at the bar, she usually had customers waiting for her.

"Who was that tall good looking guy came over to talk to you while you were playing poker last night?" Kate asked.

"You thought he was good looking? Damn, girl, your eyes must be going. Shit, that walrus mustached lawman can't hold a candle to me."

"Didn't say he was as handsome as you are, Tom my love. Just wondered who he was."

"Name is Wyatt Earp. He's a lawman from Dodge City, down here to arrest a guy who shot his wife. As you well know I cannot abide a man who would beat or shoot a woman. I promised Wyatt that I would let him know if the wife shooter came into the bar."

Tom ate a bite or two of overcooked egg, two bites of steak, kissed Kate's cheek. "See you later, Lovely Lovely." Carrying his dental case, he headed over to Dega's for a bottle of whiskey to quiet down his coughing, then strolled out to the meadow.

His first patient was a grumpy mule skinner. A large man with his bull whip still wrapped tightly around his upper arm and shoulder. He had wasted no time bathing that week or scraping the mule dirt from his boots. He had an infected lower molar. He'd carried that rotting molar in his mouth for over six months. "Rinse your mouth with this," Tom ordered as he handed the man a shot of whiskey. The man rinsed and spat the whiskey out onto the ground.

"Damn fool," said Tom. "That's good whiskey you just wasted. What in hell's the matter with you?"

When the man opened his mouth to answer, Tom grabbed the tooth, twisted it loose, heard a crack, then a pop as the molar came loose. He threw it into a glass of water.

"Damn Doc, I think you broke my jaw."

Tom looked into the man's mouth, moved his jaw, closed his jaw, looked carefully at him. "Yes, it does appear so. I fear your jaw was more severely infected than it appeared. Chew on the left side of your mouth and it should be okay in a couple of months. No extra charge for the improvement in your appearance."

CHAPTER TWO

"I been riding this here cayuse so long, I'm starting to get a hunger for oats," said Macallan. "There is little in this life we lead more exciting than ten days of eating dust and watching half-dead sagebrush and mesquite slowly drift past. By the fourth day of that last patrol, I's hoping some 'paches would attack, just for a change of scenery. I figure if they lifted my hair at least my head would be cooler. This is all your fault, Bogar. If you hadn't sugar-tongued me into enlisting to see the exciting West, I'd still be eating three squares and sleeping in a soft bed. There was more excitement walking out behind the restaurant, I worked at, and sticking my head down an empty garbage can for an hour than we've seen here in the three months since we come."

"Well, you plug-ugly wall eyed mule," said Bogar, "Yourn the one supposed to have all the brains. Why didn't you talk me out of this foolishment? I's counting on you to talk me out of 'listing."

The four friends rode together in the early morning light. James Macallan, and Ham Bogar had joined the cavalry together. They came from a small New York town and the promise of western adventure had been irresistible. Macallan quickly became known as Irish, but Bogar with his hot temper and quick fists discouraged anyone from giving him a nickname or even calling him by his first name, which he had always disliked. They'd made friends with Lynn Mease, soon to be known to everyone as Mouse, then with George English, when he'd joined their company later. The fellowship of the four helped them make the boredom of the long hours at Fort Richardson bearable. Here in the northwestern corner of Texas, with its wide sweeping vistas reaching broadly across the dusty mesquite-covered plains, it was always a long ride to get anywhere. Early riding in the dark was cooler. By mid-morning there were still small wisps of clouds trying to fight back the glare, but the sun would once again win the battle. This Saturday they were going to a celebration in Jackboro. A circular posted at the fort promised an evening dance with an organ and several violins. The four cavalry men had recently finished a two week patrol. Now the promise of cold beer, good food, and fine times had brought them to town and bolstered their spirits. There would be lots of cowboys, settlers, ranchers, and certainly more soldiers. A public dance was an occasion out here. Spirits would be high. Even a traveling dentist was reported to be setting up for the day. Good news for English, whose bad tooth had bothered him all week. The dance would be sure to bring out a few pretty ladies. The saddle weary warriors wouldn't mind looking at a pretty lady or two. And hell, maybe they could even get a spin or two around the dance floor themselves.

They pulled into the livery stable in Jackboro right at ten that morning. The sun was now baking hot. Like true horsemen, they made certain their mounts would have hay and water, with shade available during the afternoon heat. While three of the men headed straight for the beer table, English searched out the dentist. There was a large tent set up with its front flaps opened, on the edge of the meadow. A line of men was formed near the tent, and English could hear the moans from others seeking dental help. Three sorry looking men, all with at least one hand holding their jaw, stood waiting ahead of him in line. The dentist was a short slim dandy, dressed in city clothes, a derby hat, and wearing a white apron, splattered with red. He was using a sturdy four-legged saloon chair as a dental office. "Extractions $3.00" read the sign.

Within fifteen minutes, an apprehensive English was seated in the chair. The dentist rinsed his tools in a large glass of pink whiskey and wiped them clean on his apron. "Open wide." He tapped the tooth, "Is that the one?" He asked as English jumped about eight inches into the air. By the time his saddle calluses had reached the chair again, the dentist was holding his bloody tooth out for George to see. "You want it?" English shook his head, the man threw it into an empty glass on the table and gave English a drink of whiskey to rinse the socket where the tooth had been. "Don't chew on that side for a week or so. You'll be as good as new. That's three dollars."

George English walked to the edge of the clearing, spit out a mouthful of blood, then sat on the ground and waited for the dizziness and pain to subside. He heard the dentist cough several times and when he looked, English saw him drink a tumbler half full of whiskey before the next patient sat down.

As the pain receded, and English could again get on his feet, he quietly built a smoke, lit it, and went off in search of his friends. A cold beer would taste pretty good. The four stood together dressed in their cavalry uniforms, drinking long cool draughts, in the shade provided by a copse of trees. They had cleaned themselves up as best they could before coming in and they looked good. In truth, they were so used to the life here in west Texas, they no longer noticed the heavy odor of the sweat-caked uniforms that they wore. The town folk noticed though, giving the men plenty of elbow room. English, with his light brown hair, was the only one of the four with a clean-shaven face as he disliked the extra heat of facial hair. The other three men proudly wore the long handlebar mustaches that was the custom of the day. The light blonde haired Macallan's mustache never looked as full as the ones sported by the dark haired Mease and Bogar.

"Boys," said English, after several schooners, "Beer is good, but let's mosey this party over to Dega's for a couple of shots to help clean my mouth out. I drink one more beer and I'll spend the afternoon out back watering trees."

"Hell, yes," agreed Mouse. "I need something with an edge to it. My gizzard wants a little more power from the liquid coming in."

Dega's bar had a reputation for serving the best rye whiskey in Texas. Actually, Dega bought whatever homemade neutral spirits he could find. Then he doctored it up by dumping in a quart or two of molasses and a couple of plugs of tobacco into each barrel. He stirred it all up, then let it sit and age for a good week or two while the tobacco worked its magic giving the concoction an appealing walnut color. When it looked perfect, he decanted it into bottles. He didn't drink it much himself, so he seldom knew what it tasted like. He usually bought ten gallon kegs of full-power corn lightning or distilled tequila for twelve dollars. He found that his customers did not distinguish between the two. By the time he cut it in half with water, added the molasses and tobacco plugs, he had less than fourteen bucks invested and could draw out sixty bottles of liquor to sell. The bottles were easier to buy now that the railroad ran all the way to Dallas, but each bottle cost another three cents. He cleared a good profit for a small amount invested. The bottles sold for two dollars each and there were twenty shots per bottle. While he made twice the profit on individual shots, he hated to fuss with the tiny glasses, so he pushed bottles when he could.

He'd had three girls working the saloon when he first set up, but he had no sense around petticoats. They treated him with scorn, seldom gave him the full cut of their earnings and soon he was deeply in love with his busiest girl. A pretty blonde-headed whore named Waco Sue. She broke his heart by running off with an Army Colonel headed east. He missed her so much that he kicked the other girls out of the bar and now was doing as well without them around. His business had dropped off a bit, but he didn't have to deal with all the bickering and fights they had caused. The piano, sitting in one corner, had not been played since the ladies left. Dega considered this an extra bonus as the girls had only known two songs, 'John Brown's Body,' and 'Golden Slippers.' He had grown to hate both tunes.

The four Army men stood together at the bar and ordered up a two-bit shot for each.

"You fellas be in town all day?" asked Dega.

"Oh hell, yes," crowed Irish. "We're here for the dance tonight. Heard it would be a real down blow."

"We got a good organist here in Jackboro and those fiddles really get everyone in a dancing mood. Anything I can get for you?"

"You got any kind of light stuff we could chew on? Like they got out east. There, they call 'em appetizers," asked Macallan.

"No food. Food is good next door. Rosa's down the street serves up Mexican food if you want that."

"The restaurant, where I worked, used to sell appetizers called escargot. They cooked 'em all up with garlic and salt and sold six of 'em for a buck. People loved 'em," said Macallan

"You don't say. Still no food, got no cook in here."

"Want to know what escargot is? It's snails," says Macallan. "They cooked up snails and sold them to those New Yorkers. And them plumb fools just ate 'em down like they's real food."

"Aw hell," says Bogar, "give me a bottle. That Irish spring jack will talk your ear off if you stand still too long."

Bogar took his bottle and sat at a table. The other three quickly joined him with glasses. Army pay was never generous and the bottle ended up being about half the price as doing shots. He listened to Irish tell a story about cleaning the stable the night before, while everyone helped themselves to his bottle. Irish had a knack for turning an amusing incident into a damn funny story, and Bogar was fond of him. By the time Macallan got to the part where he had just convinced that new sergeant that the sergeant's part of the job was to clean off the dirty shovels, they had finished the bottle.

"Time for someone else to buy," said Bogar.

English looked at Bogar. "Do you suppose he's right? Could you really sell snails to people to eat?"

"No way, you know Irish makes up the most outlandish crap just to hear hisself whistle loud. Speaking of eating, let's hit Rosa's." Mease bought another bottle and they walked the short distance to Rosa's.

English, who had a Texican sleeping in the bunk next to his, quickly became fluent in Spanish and ordered for them all. Food at the fort was beef: steaks, roasts, or ground up, with rice, or potatoes. They all loved beef, but variety sure makes anything taste better. Here there were great quantities of affordable Mexican food. They fell onto the food loaded table with gusto. Burritos, tamales, beans, and rice disappeared, washed down with large mugs of cold beer. The four had already had a grand day and were in a fine mood. They ran into friends of theirs, more soldiers, at the restaurant and were busy swapping war stories, when Mease, the card player of the group, suggested a return to Dega's, another bottle, and a nickel ante game of poker at one of the tables. They kept the stakes low and spent much of the afternoon most pleasantly. As the sun began to retreat and the powerful heat abated, their spirits were high. They could hear the band begin to warm up. Soon the dancing would start. The bar was beginning to fill up with town people who had come out for the music but stopped in for a quick drink or two before heading down to the meadow. Dega had set up a faro table in one corner and the dentist, after finishing with his patients, had come in to run it for the saloon.

English watched the dentist indulge in another large glass of whiskey before he started the faro game. Men gathered around the table and soon there were whoops of joy and groans of despair as the customers watched the cards fall. English was not thinking the clearest, but with the cost of the tooth removal, the beer and whiskey, and the loss of some funds at the poker game, he was running short of money. Like most soldiers, he believed himself to be good at poker. In truth, he was bad at cards, losing consistently, and today he had borne the brunt of the poker losses. So he mentioned the large amount of whiskey consumed by the dealer, suggested they all take a try at the board. If he could get just a few dollars up, they could head out for the dance. The dentist obviously had a cold, as he kept a large handkerchief in his hand into which he coughed, and he took frequent drinks of Dega's finest, as he ran the game. English was certain the little man could not keep a good accounting of the action on the faro table, not with all the whiskey, he'd consumed.

The faro table was always laid out in spades, from the ace to the deuce. The black color made the silver bets placed on the spots stand out. The cards were affixed to a long green piece of velvet cloth that could be rolled up when not in use. It was the card not the suit that mattered. A ten of hearts paid off just as well as a ten of spades. The cards would be shuffled and placed in the holder box. The first card pulled out was a loser and the men on that number, lost the money they bet. The second card pulled won. The house percentages came when a pair was drawn, all bets on that number lost.

After watching for a minute, English put his dollar on the ten.

"Hell," Irish says, "I'm a king," and put his buck there. The first card was pulled with a flourish and slapped hard against the faro board. The first winning card was a king and Irish won. He was up in money already and didn't really need a hit, but those who don't need usually seem to win. It always looked like Macallan's money ran lucky.

English put another dollar on ten, this time the ten was drawn. It was a good win. No need to mess with it. Still English was certain the dealer was intoxicated and he palmed another dollar, which he dropped onto his winning first dollar. The dealer immediately stopped the game and stepped around the corner of the table.

"That was a clumsy attempt, Soldier boy. Pick up your money and leave. I will give you this one mistake if you just leave."

"That money was there before unless you want to make trouble, Shorty." English unsnapped the cover to his pistol. Then held up his aggressive move when the man didn't brace him.

The dealer quietly walked from the back of the faro table to where George had placed the bet. "You see this?" He said. His hand was pointing at English's coins. English's eyes shifted to where the dealer was pointing just long enough that he didn't see the heavy Colt 45 swung from the dealer's side. That massive piece of metal hit George right behind his left ear and dropped him where he stood like a sack of wet oats.

DOC HOLLIDAY: THE HARD RIDE

The dealer held the gun on the three soldiers still standing. "Take his two dollars and drag him out of here. The game is closed to you four. Tell him he is lucky. I had every right to kill the cheating bastard."

Looking into the barrel of the Colt, held by the steady hand and steely eyes of the dealer, left the men no choice. Unhappy they were, dead they didn't want to be. Silently the men carried their friend from the saloon, laid him on the road with his back held up by the horse railing.

"Damn, English," said Irish, "Why you want to get your head knocked in for nothing? Just lay here a moment or two and we'll see you to the dance." Macallan was looking at the good they could still do here in having a jump at the dance.

Macallan had always been a big talker, most trouble came his way he dodged. Ham Bogar was the opposite. He was little at talking, but came from a stubborn heritage that let him back down from no man. He was fast with his temper, mean with his fists. Made of a stiffer darker wood, he felt his courage had been pushed down for no reason. He was shaking with the anger that swelled through him. No man had that right. In the bar, he had stood no chance with the dealer's gun drawn and cocked. A black growing anger gripped him. "Ya can't do that to a man and call it right."

The men thought he was talking about English. They were wrong.

"That sum-bitch had no call for that," said Bogar, as he drew his pistol. Let's see how he bucks back against a drawn gun. He cocked his gun and walked back through the saloon doors. The pistol fire inside the saloon was startlingly loud. A caustic cloud of black powder smoke drifted out through the doors.

Ham came crashing back through the swinging doors. His faltering legs took two steps, then gave out. He landed half on the sidewalk and half on the road. His head was canted at an unusual angle and a hole had appeared in the middle of his chest. Blood pumped rapidly, covering parts of the wooden sidewalk, soaking into the dust road, then stopped suddenly as the air gushed from Ham's lungs. He no longer moved, the bullet had blasted most of his heart out through his back.

Irish moved to him quickly and held up his head, but he was gone. He felt the strength drain out of his own body with the death of his friend. In the Cavalry, he had previously faced hostile gunfire and death, but the reality of holding his close friend in his arms as the man's life drained from him crushed the spirit inside him. He became physically ill, emptying his stomach on the road. His hands were shaking uncontrollably. But it was plain, there's no help a doctor could give Ham. He was gone.

The Sheriff had come at a run. He stopped three yards from the men. "Back up," he said to Macallan. "Even I can see that man is dead. You can't help him. Now, tell me what happened."

Irish lowered Ham's head gently, then moved back to stand beside English and Mouse. He said, "That faro dealer buffaloed our friend and chased us out of the saloon at gun point. This man went back in there and got kilt. That faro dealer is a mad dog you gotta take care of."

Sheriff Jenson ordered them, "Wait here." He entered the saloon.

Within five minutes, he returned. "Your fellow there was cheating. I got four witnesses as say he was caught cheating. Your other companion there, walked through the door with his gun in his hand. Got ten witnesses for that. Nothing to be done here. You get your horses, take your friend's body and get back to the Fort. I'll be here if Captain Miller has any questions."

CHAPTER THREE

Dr. Thomas McKay, was a rarity here in the West. He actually had a college degree and accreditation as a dentist. Most dentists this far out had little but mail-ordered tools and a sign. McKay soon discovered that he liked gambling a great deal more that pulling teeth. His quick agile brain, together with his dexterity, and skill with weapons, suited him admirably as a professional gambler. He earned a great deal more money as a gambler. Dega was paying him over a hundred bucks a week to run the faro table, at a time when average wage was thirty bucks a month. Tom spent several afternoons each week practicing with his gun. He enjoyed the challenge of working with his gun, and knew that before long, his quick fiery temper and stubborn nature, would involve him in fights. Speed was the necessary element, every fight he witnessed was decided by the speed of the antagonists. The slower man on the attack was almost always the loser. Accuracy was secondary because most bar fights happened at a distance of less than twenty feet.

DOC HOLLIDAY: THE HARD RIDE

As a boy, he had learned how to play poker from his father at their home in Valdosta, Georgia. After his mother passed away from tuberculosis, when he was a young man, he had gone to Pennsylvania for dental school. His planned future as a dentist in Valdosta ended when his doctor diagnosed him with advanced tuberculosis, his doctor recommended that he move west where the warm dry air would hopefully extend his life. Tom had stopped at New Orleans. The city was ripe with fat poker games and dandies waiting to be stripped of their ready cash, but the heavy humidity had further damaged his lungs and a new doctor had encouraged him to move further west to more arid climes.

Dallas was perfect for him, with its dry hot days and wild open attitude toward gambling. He learned faro in Dallas. Tom had only play poker before. A faro dealer in Dallas showed him the fine points of increasing the house's profit in a game that was essentially break even. He had never cheated before, but to be successful at faro one needed quick hands and a mindset that allowed cheating. He would have stayed permanently in Dallas, but during the first four months he had been forced to defend himself, six times at the faro board. The first five duels had ended with him only wounding his opponent in the hand or arm. The last gunfight, against a fast opponent, had resulted in the man's death. Tom had not had time for accuracy and had hurried his shot. His bullet had pierced the man's heart. The law had not given him any grief over the fights, but then they had banned firearms from all bars. Less than a month later, Tom almost beheaded a man during another altercation. He'd been carrying his Arkansas Toothpick on a lanyard around his neck. Kolb Sanders had accused Tom of cheating and leaped at him with a knife. Tom's speed succeeded in defeating his opponent, but Sanders, a popular man in the still new town of Dallas, was severely mutilated. Tom was advised that a warrant for his arrest was being issued and he fled the East Texas jurisdiction followed closely by Texas Rangers and bounty hunters. Law in many of the newer territories was based more on the popularity of the victim than on written law.

Tom had settled in Jackboro, outside the influence of East Texas law. Here he was doing fine. The town was rough hewn but growing rapidly. Dirt or mud streets, depending on the rainfall, hitching posts, horse watering troughs, and wooden sidewalks just starting to be built. Only one block completed so far, but finished on both sides of the street. Naturally they had built the sidewalk in front of Dega's first, the main saloon and the only two story building in town. Next to the saloon was a restaurant. Simple menu, eggs and beef in the morning, steak, beans, and potatoes in the afternoon. A weather worn sign over the door read, 'FOOD' in faded letters. Across the street and down the block was Rosa's, a Mexican eatery. Next to Rosa's stood the hardware/general store.

Horses and mules were tied at the water troughs. Dogs ran freely through the streets. One heard the braying of donkeys and the crowing of roosters. Several houses on the outskirts of town had penned hogs, which grunted and squealed during the afternoon heat. A very definite earthy odor drifted through the heavy air after one of the rare rains.

Tom liked the climate here in West Texas. He lived in a room above the saloon and ran a relatively clean game. Over the last twelve months, he had only been involved in three shootings, with only one fatality. Sheriff Jensen understood, too well, the dangers associated with gambling. This small town on the edge of civilization saw the evil tempered buffalo hunters, aggressive soldiers, cowboys too long on the trail and hell-bent for looking for trouble, and other rowdy elements who loved to drink and gamble. Jensen liked Tom as he avoided gun play as long as possible. Tom's reputation as a fast gun helped keep much of the trouble to loud talk.

Tonight, Tom recognized the one soldier as he walked in, he had removed a tooth from him earlier. He knew this group of Army men had been in town all day and drinking more alcohol than they were used too. He always kept tight reins on his table and had immediately seen the palmed dollar coin drop. When the Soldier flipped the top of his holster open, Tom knew he was looking to buck the tiger. Tom picked his pistol up from where it was kept hidden, on a shelf, behind him as he meekly stepped around the table. When he distracted the man with his left hand, his speed in swinging the pistol ended the confrontation with the man on the floor. Once he had driven the four intoxicated Soldiers from the saloon, he walked over to the wall, just right of the door, and waited with his pistol drawn and cocked, watching the door. When the hot-headed Cavalry man ran back into the bar to attack him, Tom shot him mid-chest at about three feet. He knew he had killed the man.

He returned to the faro table, replaced his pistol on the concealed shelf, poured himself a half full glass of whiskey, drank it neat, and resumed the game. Within minutes, Sheriff Jenson crashed through the doors, leaving them to swing. Dega came from behind the bar with his hands held out in front of him. "Sheriff, Tom had no choice. He's only protecting himself. That Soldier was aiming to kill him. He came into the room with his gun out and cocked. Good thing Tom was ready for him. He had no other choice. Sheriff, you can ask any man in here. Tom was just defending himself."

Sheriff Jenson turned to Tom, "That how it was, son?"

"I fear that poor man was born with an excess of pride which had begun to weigh too heavily on his soul. He must have been looking for someone to help him with his burden. I was merely attempting to help him."

"Well, Tom," said the Sheriff. "That's your second killing in my town and I don't like it. I can see you did the best you could this time. But one more killing and I'm going to have to run you outta town. You hear me?"

"I hear, Jenson."

The next morning, Tom woke early. Someone was beating on his door. He sat up, took his pistol from under his pillow and walked to the door.

"What is it?"

"This is Jenson. Just got notified that the Army is coming for you. Better let me in."

Tom opened the door, letting the Sheriff enter. "I just heard from the telegraph operator that the Army sent a message to the Governor to have the Texas Rangers pick you up. There's a squad of Soldier boys coming in for you now. You best get dressed and packed up quick. As far as I can see you did the right thing, but this is still Texas, so you gotta step quick. I will try to help you if you stay, but them wild bastards are after blood and they could run roughshod over my jurisdiction.

31

Your neck could be six inches longer by the time I prove you innocent. I would suggest the best course of action for you is to flee. And now would be the best time for that."

"Store's closed, John. If I give you the money, would you get me some coffee, biscuits and bacon, and a couple of boxes of rifle ammo from the store. They won't say it's stolen if the Sheriff is getting it. I'll pack up and get a horse?"

"Okay," said Jensen, "Meet you out back of the bar in ten minutes."

Tom bought four bottles of whiskey, from the saloon, to take on the trip, leaving his money on the bar. He packed his few belongings at his room, headed to the livery where he gave the owner twenty five bucks for a pack horse. The livery owner had recommended a tall buckskin. He claimed the horse was sound, strong, and a good ride. Tom went with the man's suggestions, and got the horse with a saddle for another sixty-five. He lead them back and had them tied up behind the saloon, when the Sheriff came out of the store with a bag of food and ammo he threw to Tom.

"Twenty will cover it," said Jensen.

As Tom threw him the money, he heard the horses drumming loudly down Main Street, just one level of buildings away.

Sheriff Jenson said, "Damn, that sounds like the Cavalry. I was hoping you could beat them out of town. Best head north. South and west is where the army is and they'll be looking for you there, I know back east in Dallas they still got warrants out for you, but I always ignored them. I've drawn this rough map for you, may help you some. Watch for the rivers, stay north as much as you can. Little good weather would be a blessing. It'll be a tough ride, but ya better head for Denver. You'll see 900 miles of desolation and hostile Indians, but Denver is still your best bet. Good luck, son. I'm going out to try and slow them down."

"You been a good friend, Jensen. Please tell Kate to meet me in Denver. I figure it will take me a month to get there. She can make it in a week or so if she takes the train east and then north."

"Don't know her."

"She's the pretty whore down at Dega's. She's the one with the big nose. I have come to be fond of her attitude. Give this note to Wyatt Earp, that lawman from Dodge City. It has the name and address of that woman killing lowlife on it."

Tom broke the window of a shack behind the saloon. He threw a handful of shells in the room to attract attention. Then he lit the lantern hanging by the door, threw it in the broken window, and when the flames took hold, he lead his horses down the side street away from the fire.

Sheriff Jensen ran back from the street and began to shout, "Fire, Fire." as the flames grew larger. When the rounds began going off, he cautiously moved around the corner and began directing people from there. From two blocks away, Tom could see the soldiers forming up with the town people for a bucket brigade line to help save the town. Tom mounted and rode off into the dark.

Tom took the rough cut road north for twenty miles, then broke off to the northwest and pushed the buckskin up to a cantor. He rode nice, felt smooth, Tom was pleased with his choice of horses. He would have preferred a darker color, that would not have been so readily visible in the early morning or evening twilight, but the buckskin was still a fine animal. He was unsure of where Texas jurisdiction ended, but he doubted either the Army or the rangers would pursue him past the Red River. He slowed Buck to a walk and moved forward , toward a new life and the rough uncharted territory.

CHAPTER FOUR

Captain J. J. Miller, executive officer, acting commander until Colonel Braggs's replacement showed up, was awakened early with the bad news that one of his Cavalryman had been killed in town that night. He had ordered the three men who reported the death of Private Ham Bogar, brought to his office. They entered slowly, saluting the Captain and then removing their hats.

"Stand at ease. Private English, tell me what occurred in Jackboro last night relating to the death of Private Bogar. I want it straight and I want to know why my fort does not have that trained Cavalryman any longer."

"We were chased out of Dega's saloon by the faro dealer. He had us at gunpoint. There was no arguing. Private Bogar became very angry and went back into the saloon. The faro dealer shot him as he entered the door. Ham , that is Private Bogar never had a chance. The Sheriff backed the actions of the faro dealer and told us to bring Private Bogar's body back to the fort. He also said if you had any questions to talk to him."

"So if I am to believe what you are saying, you three did nothing to back Private Bogar's play."

"There was no time, Captain. Everything happened too fast."

"Fast, slow, backwards, or forwards, you are Cavalrymen, you've been trained to back each other no matter what. I am disappointed in all three of you. Gentlemen, you are dismissed. Tell my Adjutant to come in, please."

The Captain was writing a message as the Adjutant came into the office. Captain Miller sealed it in an envelope, handed it to the Adjutant, "take that into the telegraph office in town. Tell the operator it's priority and for his eyes only."

"Yes Sir," said the man as he turned to go.

"First, find Sergeant Samuels and send him in."

"Yes Sir, right away, Sir."

The Captain sat back and made his plans. He could not afford the loss of trained Cavalrymen to the rough element in town. Time to set an example. He needed to show the townsmen who ran this part of the country. He turned to face Sergeant Samuels as he entered his office.

"Sergeant, I want you to take six men, draw rations and ammo for a three days patrol. Go into town tonight and arrest the faro dealer, I believe his name is McKay. Take Privates, English, Macallan, and Mease. They will provide identification. Bring him back to the fort, if McKay resists, shoot him down where he stands. If he has run, follow him for as long as he is in federal territory. Here," he handed Samuels a paper, "This will give you permission to draw more rations and ammo at any fort, if needed. Good luck, good hunting. I want that man taken."

CHAPTER FIVE

Leaving Jackboro before the early morning sun, Tom held a course straight north following a dusty little used wagon trail. The trail had been laid following a rocky ridge that ran most of the way from Jackboro to the Red River. He rode Buck at a gentle canter that ate miles. He was well pleased with the gentle rocking gait of his new horse. He had want to buy a brown to brown-black color. He had always been told to get a darker colored animal because they were less visible from early evening through early morning. Visibility was a worry traveling through hostile territories. But this lighter colored buckskin seemed tough, and had a good spirit. The pack horse, carrying less than fifty pounds, followed easily and the trio moved at a good pace. In addition to Tom's supplies, the horse carried oats to supplement their diet, a little extra energy on the long trip.

Tom consulted his compass and watch frequently. He held a strict regimen of a ten minute break every ninety minutes wanting to ensure that Buck wouldn't be exhausted if Tom needed speed. With four hours behind them, neither horse showed any signs of distress.

At each break, Tom stopped at the highest accessible point on the road. He would indulge in the traditional travelers rest by building a smoke and taking the time to enjoy it before moving on.

He watched his back trail for movement. On his third break, he saw dust plumes rising and assumed that the animals causing the dust were carrying men hunting him. Few others would ever move so rapidly in the morning heat. By his calculations, he was ten miles from the Red River and safely now. The group behind him appeared to be at least two miles behind him. At the next hard section of road, he pulled his horse sharply to the left. The animal jumped half-way down the eight foot bank, stumbled in the loose shale, then regained his footing and responding to Tom's heels, ran westward at a faster rate of speed. He easily navigated through the sparse vegetation. Tom headed west for several miles before returning to his northern route. The ride down through the mesquite and cacti on the hard packed ground would slow the pursuit. Maybe throw his pursuers off course all together.

He reached the Red well before actually seeing his pursuers. The river ran wide here, two hundred yards of moving water but only two to three feet deep. Tom knew the dangers of quicksand were present with water that shallow and fast. He had never ridden across a river before and would have avoided the crossing if possible, but the pursuers were closing in. He had to get out of Texas. He began walking the buckskin into the water. The coolness of the breeze blowing over the river was welcome. He gave his animals a couple of minutes to drink. The horses had no fear and surged forward with no difficulty. Tom relaxed and even began to enjoy the ride by the time he had reached the other shore. He rode the horses another thirty yards past the bank, tied them to a cottonwood tree in the deep shade where they could cool off. He ran back to the edge of the river with his Winchester and found an excellent defensive position. This avoiding pursuit was beginning to eat at Tom's craw. These sons-of-bitches were trying to catch and hang him. He might just as well get hung for killing a couple more.

He had an open field of fire in front of him. His pursuers needed to cross two hundred yards of open water. If they attacked en masse, he would have time to kill them all. As he watched, they came to the bank of the river and stopped. They all dismounted and watered their horses while they stood in full sun light on the sandy bank. It was a squad of six Cavalryman and a man with long black hair dressed in civilian clothes. Clearly there was an argument raging amongst them. One man pulled out a map and demonstrated something on it, but the argument was loud and raged on. Finally, the man dressed in civilian clothes got on his horse and began to cross the river. Tom believed this man to be the tracker. He shot the man's horse in the chest at about one hundred yards and watched as the man was thrown from his back. Tom pulled his Winchester around to take a shot at another horse, but the others were quickly leading their horses out of range. The horse, he had hit, thrashed around but the currents pull forced him downstream. The man regained his footing and began to work his way back to the south bank Tom put two more rounds through the tree limbs over their heads. Then he ran for his horses and quickly rode north again. He figured they would palaver a bit, then some would follow, maybe all would follow, but they would be slower without that horse. If he was their tracker, that would slow them considerably, as he was sure none of the Cavalrymen would voluntarily give up his mount to an Indian, even if he was a tracker. He expected to gain at least two hours before they regained his trail.

CHAPTER SIX

Now that he had moved into the Indian Territory he reverted to his birth name, John Holliday. The East Texas warrant had no more power here than the West Texas warrant had now for Tom McKay. Might as well be yourself when you can.

Ahead of him now, Doc could see an unbroken ridge rising five hundred feet into the air. Stopping and resting Buck, Doc slowly constructed a tailor made, lit it, inhaled deeply. He coughed, pulled the whiskey bottle from his pack, and took a good long drink to ease his throat. "Johnny, you are going to have to cut back on the tobacco. Funny," he thought, "No one but Ma ever called me that. God, I miss that woman." He looked closely at the banked ridge that faced him . It had risen unbroken and solid from a buckling of the earth eons ago and had been forced to endure the weather here in the southwest. Heat, wind, rain, and cold had worked their magic on what would have been an impossible climb at one time. Now, it had a broken face with gullies, washes and animal trails running across its front. The difficulty for Doc was that a trail which appeared promising from below could vanish half-way to the mesa.

He saw what looked to be an opening flaw in the high mesa edge and decided that tiny crack would be his best option. All his life, John Holliday had believed in his own decisions. He lived with them and took the hit or the profit each had brought him. A gambler to his core, he analyzed the data and realizing if he made the wrong choice here it could cost him his life, took what he felt was the best option. Trust in his own judgment had long been a necessary part of his survival.

The journey upwards began easily. Climbing through the aromatic sage and twisted cedars, the ground was soft but Buck was sure-footed and climbed easily. Too soon the trail turned to red rock and shale. The animals slowed and Doc was forced to dismount and lead them at a careful walk. It was difficult to see how far he had climbed because of the thick vegetation growing high on the previous rock falls and landslides. Two hours into the climb, Doc led the horses out into the open and could see a wide vista spread below him. Perhaps one hundred feet were left to climb. Again he rested the animals and his own aching legs. Looking out he realized he might be the first man ever to stand here and see this beautiful panorama spread before him. For the first time, Doc realized the beckoning beauty of the western expanse and felt its pull.

Turning back to his task at hand, he scanned the distance left, could see little solid footing ahead. There was a game trail leading upward about thirty yards east of him. It looked to be a difficult, but possible passage. Now was not a time to look down or back. Doc hoped the trail had been made by deer or buffalo not mountain goats. He worked his way east and began slowly to climb. He paused after each step, allowing time for the horses to secure good footing before proceeding.

DOC HOLLIDAY: THE HARD RIDE

He held the reins to Buck in his left hand, the pack horse was tied to Buck's saddle. His right hand held the knife. If the horses didn't make it, he could not let them pull him down the bluff face. Barely ten feet from the mesa floor, he slipped, fell face down on the path. He drove the knife hard into the scrabble surface and it held. He laid still for a moment to regain his breath and then stood. He saw two good foot holds ahead and jumped for them. With two quick steps he was up off the floor of the mesa and Buck, that magnificent sure footed beast scrambled up easily. The pack horse would have been lost, but Buck's strength pulled him up over the rim. Doc walked the horses thirty yards back from the edge to a small cottonwood tree. Secured the horses to it, unloaded the pack animal and took Buck's saddle off. He fanned both animals with the blanket trying to cool them off faster. He rubbed both down when he finished. His life now was closely tied to the survival of these two dumb animals.

Taking his Winchester, he walked back to the rim of the mesa. He saw three pursuers coming toward him, still distant from the foot of the bluff, and snapped off a quick shot at them. He knew they were too distant to hit them, but felt that perhaps it would worry them and slow their climb up the side of the bluff. "I doubt you slowed them much, Johnny," he thought as he saddled Buck, reloaded the pack horse and set off across the mesa.

He held the animals to a slower gait for the next five hours, several times he dismounted and walked to conserve the strength of his animals. The one-eyed heat beast was slowly losing her grip as the light softened. Long shadows began to play tricks on Doc's

43

eyes. Where before only flat mesa had been visible, now small bushes and slight gullies appeared. It had been a hard day of sun and bone-weary riding by the time he slid off Buck's back in the meager shade of a pinion pine. Still even the slight shade provided by the weather beaten tree help ease the heat a little. Doc was not a horseman. His previous travels had been by stagecoach or train. He knew how to ride, but had never used a horse to cross long distances. His legs and buttocks unaccustomed to long hours in the saddle were rubbed raw. Doc pulled Buck's saddle off. He walked around stretching his legs easing some of the pain in his lower back from the long day in the saddle. His own pain reduced a little, he rubbed Buck's back and legs down with the blanket. Then tied Buck to the tree by the reins and began to construct a cigarette. The paper and tobacco were a little damp from sweat so extra care was needed to complete a smoke. Firing it up, he walked around the tree, looking in all directions, loosening up his legs, and worrying about pursuers and Indians. He began to cough violently as his body reacted to the tobacco. He searched out the whiskey and took a long pull to quiet his lungs.

Close as he could figure, the troopers were at least three hours back. When he stood watching this morning out over the prairie from the top of the mesa, he saw the three soldiers follow his trail to the base of the mesa wall. The steep trail had required him to dismount and lead his horse up the trail. Buck was sure-footed, but it had still taken him three hours to climb to the high plateau. The long uphill climb left him and Buck exhausted. He had walked for several hours during the day and assumed the Cavalrymen need to walk to conserve their mounts also. Buck had to be ready to run long and fast if hostiles discovered them. His pursuers may have made it up faster being as they were trained Cavalrymen, but he was sure he would be at least several hours ahead of them. The lack of water for the last two days must be a hardship for their horses as well as his. No sign of Indians as yet, but he knew to keep a constant vigil for them with his slow speed.

Looking ahead, a prairie dog colony stretched out at least a half mile in each direction. It was a real quandary for him. No good choice to make, going around was longer miles on tired animals, leading them through on foot was dangerous with the numerous visible holes which if stepped into would break the horses leg. Their weight could collapse a shallow tunnel with disastrous results. He decided he couldn't risk it, going around was a must. "What do you think Buck? Which way you want to go?" The horse turned and looked at him. "Yes I agree, Buck, you do know more than me, I should have asked you before." He stripped his cigarette, letting the paper and tobacco blow away with the breeze. No sense in leaving anything extra to show his presence. He walked out into the colony and sat for a few minutes. Soon the friendly little animals were crowding him to see what he was doing. He harvested two with his knife, cleaned and skinned them out in the colony, and stored them on the pack horse. He saddled his mount, held the leash to his pack animal and rode into the setting sun. West would give him a few extra minutes to find a place to camp for the night.

Luck rode with him. In less than two miles, the prairie dog colony ended and he pointed Buck north again. As the early twilight began to paint the mesa with purples and grays, he found his way blocked by a dense chaparral. Again he turned west, following the edge of the growth, looking for a depression or a break in the dense thorny bushes where he could set up a camp and have a fire. Out on the mesa, a lone fire with a rising smoke trail was a welcoming sign to any hostiles around. "Come on in and get me, I am alone and don't know what I'm doing."

Less than twenty minutes later, a large muley deer broke cover in front of Doc and high kicked away from view. Deer tend to stay close to the heavy growth for shelter and water. They seldom moved more than three miles from water. Doc dismounted where the big buck broke cover, searching for a game path that might lead to water. He saw where the heavy vegetation parted, just a bit, and with a lot of pulling, tugging, and swearing at Buck, finally got the animals to follow him into that slight part. They headed into the heart of the chaparral. Within a half a mile, he found a small rivulet in a small opening of the brush. He let his animals drink deeply , then removed their saddle and packs. The opening made by deer trying to get water, had been widened by their grazing and sleeping. It was only ten feet wide, but it would serve nicely to hide his fire, break up the smoke, and protect him for the night. The horses would hear anything approaching and give him warning.

He soon had a small fire going with coffee boiling. The prairie dogs on a spit, gave of a delicious aroma and Doc found he was famished. The half-burned little critters went down just fine with a

46

couple of biscuits. He rubbed down Buck and the pack horse, filled the canteens for tomorrow, tied his lariat across the break in the opening to let his horses have enough room to get to the edible plants. He doubted they would wander down the thorny entrance to the mesa during the night, but still best to make sure your mount will be there in the morning. He fired him up another smoke. He had a wracking cough, spit out some blood, and took a large mouthful of whiskey to sooth his throat. He stripped down and bathed his buttocks and inner thighs in the creek, then rubbed a palm full of whiskey into the raw areas to help them heal faster. The raw acid pain made him dance for several minutes. "Damn," he thought, "the tuberculosis is getting worse, my legs and back hurt, and I'm not that sure my whiskey will hold up. Bet this is why my Pappy never took me camping." He settled down by the little campfire trying to get comfortable for the long night ahead. He poured a large whiskey into his coffee and settled back. The hard ground was poor substitute for the soft beds Doc was used to sleeping on, but the day's physically demanding ride let him sleep soundly if uncomfortably.

The sky was streaking yellows and reds when Doc awoke. He started the coffee, had a hard tack biscuit, and began to roll the morning smoke. Today would be another sun fired day and early traveling was easier on the animals. He lit his cigarette and began coughing. Several long pulls of his bottle were needed to quiet the spasm. He had repacked the horse and was beginning to saddle Buck when he heard the gun fire. The distinct bark of a Spencer told him that Army guys had gotten themselves into a pretty good little fracas. Other than military, there were few Spencers this far west. An Indian hunting party had probably found them. The sounds were close. His pursuers had followed him faster and longer that he had estimated.

"Well, this fight would give him a little more lead," He thought. Pouring himself another cup of coffee and settling back. He had been worried about running into Indians, now here they were, making his life easier by slowing his pursuers down.

By the time he finished his coffee and broke his camp, he knew he had to go back to help them. The fight had been going for a good piece of time. Holliday wanted his pursuers held up not killed. They were white men, after all, in hostile territory, if taken by the Kiowas, their deaths would take days of unrelenting pain. There was an unwritten bond of race, known to every southerner. He would, if circumstances required, face and kill his pursuers to prevent his being taken prisoner, but to abandon them to a slow horrible death was against his strong moral code. In a world of we's and them's, he still had to back the we's. A further consideration was he could end up getting the brunt of the blame, if they were killed. He tied his pack animal to the mesquite bushes and led Buck back out of the chaparral. He kicked the horse up to a rapid ground eating canter back toward the sound of gun fire. He saw no movement as he neared the sounds of the battle. Closer still, he came to a clear break in the ground, an arroyo leading down off the mesa, dismounting he cautiously led Buck down by his reins. Studying the ground before him, he almost missed the faint sound of a pebble being dislodged behind him. He felt a slight breeze as a bullet went past his left cheek, then heard the roar of the rifle behind him. Whirling and throwing his knife in one motion, he caught the Kiowa brave just above his breast bone as the man entered the arroyo behind him. The Brave was cocking the rifle to fire again, but now the weapon fell from his hands. Strength and determination pushed the Indian forward and despite his mortal injury he leaped at Doc, knocking him backward down the gully. Holliday crushed heavily against the rocks beneath him. He twisted wildly attempting to shrug the heavier man from above him. Lying on a downward incline with his head lower than his feet, caused Doc's blood to rush to his head. The combination of the powerful blow and being trapped under the Brave was quickly drained his strength. The savage Kiowa grabbed at Doc's throat and with his left hand began to choke him while he pushed himself upward. The Indian pulled a knife from his boot and stabbed downward at Holliday's head. With Doc's speed and reflexes, he just managed to grab the man's wrist and stop the downward thrust. As they struggled for the knife, Holliday smashed his forehead into the hilt of the knife still embedded in his enemy's throat. Immediately he was rewarded with a spray of blood covering his face, causing him problems with breathing. He spit, choked, and gasped for air. The quantity of blood continued to impede him, almost suffocating him. As Doc felt his strength fade, the Brave collapsed on him and Doc heard the man's death rattle as the final breath slowly left the Indian's body.

With his hands now free, he cleaned his nose and mouth of the clotting blood. With a couple of deep breathes, he regained his strength and began shifting and wriggling his body trying to extricate himself from under the dead man. Once he was able to roll free and stand, Doc braced his foot on the Indian's chest and jerked his knife out. Cleaning it by thrusting it into the ground several times, he replaced it in his sheath. Leading Buck further into the arroyo, he tied the still calm horse to a small mesquite tree. He waited there for a minute to calm his shaking hands then and continued down toward the sounds of the battle.

At the end of the narrow arroyo, where it entered a wider wash, Doc could see three troopers pinned against a gully wall. They were barricaded in by several large boulder which had washed down, and smaller rocks and dirt which the men had thrown up to make their position more secure. Looking further down the wash, Doc could see the position of the Indians. Thirty yards behind them he could make out the shapes of at least six horses, their ramuda was secured by ropes. Although he had killed one hostile the hunting party had sent out to flank the men, he would need to pay close attention that more were not coming.

"Hey Army guys, I'm here to help, don't shoot at me."

"We heard that shot over there and thought they's flanking us. Glad to hear we got help. We ain't gonna shoot at you. We'll take all the help we can get. You got any water? We got a wounded man here and he needs water bad."

"Here it comes." Doc whirled his canteen over his head and threw it up against the gully wall where it hit and then slid down to the men. Doc could hear them drinking greedily.

"How long you been pinned?" he asked.

"Seems like forever, but must be just an hour. They hit us at first light and we just made it here to these boulders. We're thinking there must be at least ten of 'em. Sure glad you came by."

"What are you troops doing out here?"

"We was sent out in a search party for Tom McKay. He killed a Soldier named Bogar in Jackboro."

"Well, the bad news for you is that I'm Tom McKay?"

"You don't have to worry about us. Army sent us out here to bring you back, but we have already passed the legal point where we have any jurisdiction."

"You ain't got a prairie dogs chance of me helping you if you're still going to be chasing me. I'm not going back to Jackboro, and not planning on getting my neck stretched. What kinda stupid dolts they sending out to catch me?"

"We have exceeded our authority in coming this far. We were already heading back when these Indians attacked us. We're no longer chasing you. Going back to Texas if we live the day."

"Well let's us just talk of that for a minute. If I help you, I want your word you won't shoot me down or take me prisoner. You gotta swear to that or I'm riding."

Doc could hear them talking amongst themselves. Then one guy shouts, "Word of God from all three of us, you help us, you are totally safe from us. We was saying the truth about heading home this morning anyway."

"Get ready then, I'm going to spook their horses that should get everything moving. They'll leave or attack, don't know which. They's Kiowas though, so they probably just came to steal your horses anyway. You turn on me, I'm going to kill everyone of you, so you better keep you word. I'd make you wish them Kiowas got you."

"We're with you, mister."

"I can see where they are forted up near the base o that stand of cottonwoods. I got a pretty good angle and will start firing here in a moment. When I cut loose, you get those Spensers of yours to working 'em too. Once they break, pour it on 'em. We will rush over and see if we can get your horses back."

Carefully sighting his Winchester on the cottonwood barricade, Doc started firing, the troopers kicked in with the big rifles. Doc turned his rifle on the rocks above the Indians' horses. The ricochets and stinging pieces of flying rock startled the horses and they fought against the ropes and branch barriers holding them. One of his bullets nicked a horse and fresh blood sprayed. They reacted violently to the smell of fresh blood with terror. They made a fierce noise fighting the sides of the arroyo, the ropes, and the other horses in their attempt to gain freedom. The Indians ran to save the mounts and two of the Army men gave chase. Doc fired twice more at the fleeing hostiles and joined the chase himself. By the time he and the soldiers reached the cottonwood tree, the Indians were gone with the horses. One Kiowa Brave was lying dead with half of his head blown off. His body had been slammed up against a cottonwood tree. Now he lay crumpled beneath it with the dirt around colored red by his blood.

"I think they're gone. Come on over here. Let's get moving before they regroup." said Doc. The two men went back to their barricade and came out, helping support a third Soldier who was wounded. He had an arrow protruding from his upper belly.

Doc said, "Let's get a look at him." The arrow was lodged above his lower gut so it was possible he could survive. Holliday knew that once the gut is perforated, it turns septic fast and it's a certain painful death. With luck, this Cavalryman might live, but he will probably die from infection if we don't get that arrowhead out." Doc broke the arrow off so only a few inches extended out. "It will help him avoid driving it deeper," he said. All four crossed to the arroyo Doc came down, they hurried to where Buck was tied, loaded the wounded man on Buck, and leading the horse, Doc ran out of the arroyo and back onto the mesa. He gave the men his second canteen. "Drink, we got five miles to cover and you'll both have to run. Those Kiowas return, we're going to have a helluva donnybrook. "

He took off at a run, leading Buck. He didn't look back, knowing the men had to follow or die. They didn't know where he was going so they wouldn't back shoot him. They needed him to live. The man on the horse groaned in pain.

"Slow down a little, let's give him a break to ease his pain."

"Can't. We slow down he's dead anyway. Them Indians catch us, we're all dead. He will live another three or four hours till we get to camp and get that arrow. It's all we can do. It would be a mercy to shoot him here. I can't, but won't say nothing if you do. Do it quick though, that dust over there is either a zephyr or them Kiowas."

"Can't shoot my friend. Let's run."

They ran for a few minutes, then Doc shouted, "They's Kiowas, don't stop for nothing. We gotta get there or die." He jumped on the horse, behind the injured man, "Grab ahold of Buck's tail and put some spring in them jumps."

The Kiowas were less than four hundred yards behind them as they entered the chaparral. They turned to fire back at the Indians, while Doc ran ahead with the horse, Macallan and English laid down on their stomachs and began to return fire. Doc tied off Buck fifty yards in, then returned to help fight the hostiles off. "Make 'em come close before you fire. We gotta keep some ammo."

Once the Kiowas saw the men had a good defensive position and were not going to be easily defeated, they ceased their attack. One Indian, in turning his horse, was knocked from the animal, by a bullet that hit his shoulder. The others stopped, caught his horse up, helped there injured companion remount, and rode off.

Doc and the three Cavalrymen watched for the Indians to return. After fifteen minutes with no sign of their enemy, Doc slowly led the men into the deep chaparral slowly. The trail was too narrow for them to shoot at him without endangering the horse. Once he got to the campsite, he turned to face them.

"Better make sure you know who your friend is here."

"We still square. We know you did right."

"One more thing, said Doc, "I recognize you." Pointing at English, he said, "I pulled your tooth and caught you cheating in Jackboro. You, all three, were with the guy I killed that night. I know the Army well enough to know they wouldn't have sent you out by yourselves. So why'r you here?"

DOC HOLLIDAY: THE HARD RIDE

Doc was looking at the speaker, Macallan. He was blonde haired, six foot tall packing two hundred pounds of muscle. The other man, English was just shorter than Macallan, but looked to be the same weight. Both were wearing the government- issue uniform, holster, belt, and pistol.

Doc at five eight, weighing one fifty at best, still dressed in his faro dealer clothes, with his gun holstered and held in by a small leather thong, looked like the weak link in this chain of three. But King Colt made him more even. He was lighting fast, better heeled, and totally fearless.

"The Army sent a patrol out to capture you, but the patrol stopped at Red River when you threw those shots at us. The Army had no jurisdiction on the north side of the river. I was still burning over Ham's death, George and Lynn backed me to get you. We thought we'd catch you quick and take you back. But it can seem like nothing turns just like a guy'd think out here in the west. By the time we knew we'd made a mistake and were started back, them Indian's was on us."

"Just so you know, my real name is John Holliday. McKay was an alias. People call me, Doc."

Irish said, "I'm James Macallan. He's George English, and the injured man is Lynn Mease. "Can't say as I am all that pleased to meet y'all. We can chew this over more, later, let's see if we can save your friend's life. Let's do first things first. If we don't get that arrow out of Mr. Mease, he will be dead by morning. Either one of you want to do the arrow removing?"

"Neither of us has before, if you have some training, we'll rely on you."

"Ain't no guarantees here. If he lives it will be a miracle, but we gotta take a chance to try to save him. Are you with me on that?"

"Do your best, Mr. Holliday."

Gathering smaller branches and picking up the dead wood lying around, Doc lit the campfire. He filled the coffee pot with water and put it over the fire. Pulling out his dental bag and hunting knife, he addressed the wounded man, "What's your name, Mister?"

"I'm Lynn Mease," he croaked out.

"Well Lynn, here's the thing. We gotta get that arrow out or your wound will putrefy. That's a sure bad death. Do you understand?"

"Yep, I know you right."

Doc put the very edge of his scalpel near the fire. He put the full blade of his hunting knife directly into the flames.

"I'm a dentist, not a doctor, but I'm all you got. I will do my best to get that chunk of wood out of you." Turning his head he began talking to the other two men, "Going to need your help, men, so listen up. Take off his jacket, tear out the lining and drop the lining into the coffee pot. That's all I got for dressing this wound. And Macallan, you cut me three lengths of rope big enough to fit around his head and hold his jaw shut. Do it now and get it done fast. More speed the better here."

English removed the jacket lining and dropped it in the boiling water.

"From the smell of it, that really needed cleaning." Macallan came running up with the pieces of rope.

DOC HOLLIDAY: THE HARD RIDE

"Unravel them down till you get about six stands," Said Doc.

"Lynn, I want you to know why I'm doing this. I am going to cauterize that wound to keep it from rotting. It's going to hurt but we can't let you scream or we'll be fighting hostiles in the middle of the arrow removal." He wrapped a strand of the rope around the man's head and tied it, holding the man's jaw shut.

"Hold him down, boys. Macallan, raise his arms up over his head. English, sit on his legs. Try to hold him as still as you can, cause here we go." He could feel the fear grow in Lynn. Doc knew he needed to start before Mease's fear became uncontrollable. Doc used the scalpel first, cutting down the shaft of the arrow, enlarging the hole, making sure that the arrowhead was free. Then laying the scalpel down, he picked up the glowing red hunting knife. "Now's the hard part. Hope you trust me, Lynn, cause I believe we can get you through this."

With his free hand, he covered the man's mouth and held his nose shut. Mease squirmed and tried to get free, trying to prevent his suffocation. Then his body lifted off the ground in an intense spasm as he passed out. Holliday let go of his nose, jerked the arrow out and thrust the blade of the knife deep into the wound. Dark acrid smoke came from the wound as he twisted it, making sure all sides were cauterized. He pulled the knife out, set it back in the fire, and began to sew the wound together. Lynn regained consciousness during the sewing but the greatest amount of pain had passed. Doc poured whiskey on Mease's stomach to cleanse it, dressed the wound with the hot cloth from the coffee pot. He tied the rough lining to Mease with a stretch of rope, then released the rope tied around his head.

"Damn," said Doc. "That was harder than I thought. Hope I never have to go through that again."

"I thought you'd kilt him dead," said English.

"We'll know by morning. It's a bad place to get hit. I saw a drowned child brought back to life once and thought that if he was unconscious for a short time, it might work to cut out some of his pain. I'm only a dentist, but it looks like it worked. We'll see what the sunlight brings," said Doc.

Doc looked over the two standing men while he pulled out his papers and tobacco, started building a smoke. "Let's talk a little about what you are planning."

"How far you reckon to a real doctor for Lynn?" asked English.

"I've never been this way before so I'm figuring closest is Fort Richardson. That's about 150 miles back for you. Bad part of that's there may be a rope waiting for you to dance on. Denver is probably 700 miles ahead. Sure they got a doctor there, but Mease will be recovered or dead by then," said Doc.

"Don't appear to be a pleasant time ahead," said Macallan. "Why do you think there may be a rope waiting for us?"

"The Red River War is still a declared war. You, all three, became deserters when you left that patrol. You had to be disobeying orders at that time because your Commanding Officer wouldn't have sent you out of Federal territory. You go back now, your C.O. might ignore it, or you might get hung. Chew it over, if you want to throw in with me, we're heading for Denver. I got no choice. You want to head back, stay the night, I'll help you boys with that pack horse to pull Lynn's sled, one canteen, and some grub. After that, you're on your own. Gotta tell you now though, either way seems a toss up to me. We all got some hard riding ahead."

Doc watching both men, did not sense any aggression toward him. The two walked back to the stream to drink.

"Didn't know a man could get that dry and live," Macallan said. "Another hour without water and I'd have blown away on the breeze."

The two men sat by themselves near the creek, speaking quietly, they rolled smokes, looked long at each other, talked in low tones. Doc left them by themselves so as to not influence the action they would take the next day. He never relaxed his vigil of their actions though. He didn't trust them as yet. Two men talking quietly by themselves does not foster a strong feeling of trust in a third man watching.

Doc put on a pot of water for coffee. Thoughtfully building another smoke, he inhaled, coughed loudly into his handkerchief, looked at the new spray of blood. He took a long drink off his whiskey bottle to calm his throat. He knew smoking was further injuring his lungs, but he still had plenty of whiskey to hold the coughing down. He watched the men for some longer, then wandered down the path to make sure the Kiowas weren't coming back on them. Halfway down the walk to the mesa, Holliday stopped and stepped off the path backing into the heavy foliage. He listened closely for sounds of them following him. He had always been cautious and knew talk was too frequently only noise made to expedite the moment. These men had pursued him. They had a blood grudge against him. If they were coming for him, he would make sure he ended this trail alone. After a year as a professional gambler, the loneliest profession on earth, Doc trusted no one. He had few friends and many enemies. Every instinct told him to just kill the three. They would never be found here in the deep chaparral. He knew he could easily dispatch the two, still he knew killing the wounded man would be difficult. He trusted English deep within himself, but Macallan was a loose talker. He could say all the right things and appear to be trustworthy, but there was a darkness in him. He would have liked to know what the men said back at the campsite. Doc hearing nothing, checked out the mesa, then returned to the creek. He watched carefully coming into camp. Both men had helped themselves to a cup of coffee. The aroma filled the small campsite. They were looking for him, neither appeared to be threatening.

English took the lead. "We've decided to throw in with you. Truth is, you had no choice with Bogar. I'd of shot him if he came back through the doors with his pistol cocked to kill me. You's right. Also, I want to say I'm grateful for this morning. Those bronze-skinned heathens had us dead in another hour. We are with you for the duration. What you said made sense. We'd be proud to accompany you to Denver."

"He is saying what we decided and I'm agreeing. Further, if we give our word, we will stand by it", said Macallan.

DOC HOLLIDAY: THE HARD RIDE

"Gents, we got a hard time coming, but let's eat, drink as much water as we can and rest up for a day of traveling. We leave early in the morning. Hopefully we can shake those Kiowas off our ass and travel a good distance before we need to rest. We got four men and two horses. That spindle-legged pack horse ain't worth much, but he will handle the supplies and pull a drag sleigh with the injured man on it. That leaves you two walking but we'll take all the water we can carry and, hell, we might make it. Doc cut up some bacon, put it on the fire, broke out some hard tack to chew on, then cracked open the cork on a bottle of whiskey. "Here's to good times," He took a good slug and threw the bottle to Macallan. He drank deeply and handed it to English.

"By good times, I mean we are all still breathing. It's wonderful," said Doc.

"Four men with steel resolve can do anything," said Macallan. "We are committed, we can do it."

"Just tell me one thing now as we're partners," Said English.

"Sure, whatcha wanna know?"

"How did you know those hostiles where Kiowas?"

"That was my best guess. I figure the Apache are further west. They are mean bastards, but the Army is chasing them too hard for them to come this far east. It's possible they were Ute or Arapahoe, but they look like that Kiowa scout that used to hang out in Jackboro. I knew they wasn't Comanche's, I wouldn't have heard the fight. They would have had you tied up and been frying up your testicles for breakfast while you watched. Then they'd have cut out your eyes and turned you loose to wander, blind, and bleeding till you died. Not much tougher or meaner in this world than a Comanche warrior."

CHAPTER SEVEN

Watchful and uneasy, Holliday, was first up in the morning. His cough produced a small amount of blood, he used the whiskey to soothe his throat. Starting a small fire, soon he had a pan of water and a handful of coffee cooking. English started securing the load on the pack animal, while Holliday was getting Buck ready for the day. All four men poured a little coffee and sat quietly munching on hard tack biscuits. They broke out tobacco and papers to roll the first of the day. Silently the small group contemplated the difficulty inherent in the day that lay ahead. Macallan built an extra for Mease who was still feeling poorly. The fragrant odor of four smokes filled the small campsite. A travois had been built for Mease out of two long branches and bed woven out of the pieces from the unraveled lariat.

"Macallan, you and English tote that drag sleigh to the mesa for Mease. I'll lead the animals. Mease, you gotta get up and walk. I know it will be bad painful, it will feel like you're walking into hell itself, but you have to do it yourself. If you can't do it now, you never will be able to and there is no sense in us dragging a dying man along. Your bloods gotta move, your body has to start working."

Mease struggled to stand, his face white with pain. Macallan hurried to help his hurting friend. Holliday stopped him. "If he wants to live, he's going to count on himself, not you."

"You a mean bastard, Doc, but don't wait none on me. I know I can make it myself," said Mease, as he finally stood straight and took several halting steps.

The two hale cavalry men walked the game trail to the chaparral opening. Following was Holliday leading the horses. The men stood quietly together in the cool morning air, looking for any sign of their enemy in the weak morning light. No sign of any Kiowas, but Holliday could feel the resentment against him in the air. When Mease struggled up the half mile to the opening, they helped him into the travois.

"How you feeling now?"

"I'll live."

"Alright then, we're off to Denver," said Macallan. "Let the women beware." Holliday kept Buck to a walk pointing him west following the dark line of the chaparral. He held the reins to the pack horse in his hand. Macallan and English brought up the tail of the struggling little band.

The sun's first glance over the edge of the horizon found the men stumbling over the terrain. Threads of gold mixed slowly with pale yellows and streaks of polished vermillion began a majestic show in the eastern sky. Slowly as the light increased, the trailing men made better time as they now could make out the obstacles hidden by the dark. A slight chill hung over the vast mesa. As pleasant as the walk began, the men knew the temperature would soon rise. They kicked up several deer and while they hungered for the food, it was too early in the day to harvest any additional weight.

The mesa floor was alive with small chirping birds. They complained loudly at the intruders and then moved just enough to let the men and horses pass. There were many wrens, and a few squawking jays, raucous in their irritation at being disturbed.

The sun seemed to suddenly mushroom out rapidly. The heat began to paint dark wet blotches on the men's clothing. The birds left with the heat, seeking new hunting grounds deep in the shade of the thick chaparral.

Buck leading the way seemed happy with the travel. He began to prance wanting to move at a faster pace than the enforced slowness of the march. Holliday struggled to keep him to a walk. Macallan and English walked out to the sides avoiding the alkaline dust stirred slightly by the horses. Once kicked up, it hung in the air low and long after the animals passed. It was irritating to noses and lungs, and clung to lips and eyelids. Soon the two walkers covered their lower faces with bandannas.

They walked in silence for the first thirty minutes, all eyes constantly moving, searching the mesa for any evidence of the Indians. Then Macallan couldn't stand the quiet any longer.

"I ever tell you galoots how I ended up way out here? Thing is back in the Grand country where my family hails from, we were land owners and very successful, too successful as it turns out."

"If it was all that grand, why did you leave it?" asked English.

"I'm getting there, I'm getting there. You gotta be a little patient.""I'm toasting my testicles here, I'm not in a mood for patience."

"Well anyway, one day God called St. Patrick in for a little talk."

"Okay, okay, I see this is one of your stories. I never did figure your history led back to nobody with money," said English.

"You could stop interrupting me. 'St. Pat,' says God, 'these Macallans down in Dublin are accumulating too much wealth. I want you to go down there and tell them they have to move to London. I feel the English could use a little good Irish humor. The Macallans would be the perfect people to spread humor amongst those grumpy people and have to work a little harder to get more wealth.' Well, my great-great-great granddad said 'I'd rather be sent to hell.' So that's how we ended up in New York. Of course, I didn't realize it at the time, but that was just the first step. When I volunteered for the cavalry in Texas I was completing the journey."

"What in the hell you talking about, good Irish humor? I know Apaches tell better jokes than the Irish."

"You'd both be wise to use your ears and save your breath for now," said Holliday. "Talking will dry you out faster. If you find a small hard stone, suck it, it will help relieve some of the dryness and keep your tongue from swelling." While English and Mease had liked the story, they knew Holliday to be right. Macallan as always was irked by the rebuke. It was a long dry trip ahead whether he told a story or not. Seemed that Holliday was always riding his ass unnecessarily. The sun now blazed with a bright white heat. By dusk they were all weary as a three legged dog. The cavalry had never been known for long hikes. Irish Macallan and George English's legs were complaining bitterly of the unaccustomed use. The heat had cooked them all dry. When they set up camp, Irish suggested they split one canteen and save the second for the next day.

Holliday took off his hat with one hand, and sleeved his face dry with his arm."It has frequently astounded me how some men would ration out other peoples things. Usually they set up a committee but I see Mr. Macallan has taken up the post all by himself. I believe the water in my canteens is mine. What say you, Mr. Macallan?

"Of course it's yours, Doc. Why you so contrary about it, it was only a suggestion. Why you always seeming to bite at me?"

"You seeming to want to run things here, MaCallan. Should face up pretty quick that no one runs me. Especially a mouthy little bastard like you. When you get that, maybe you will get on better. But in the meantime, I will decide how much and when my stuff will be rationed, if it's rationed at all." Holliday split the canteens giving half a canteen to each man. "This way, we'll sleep better and feel more refreshed for the walk tomorrow. As dry as we are, our bodies need the water and won't waste it," said Holliday. "With luck, the horses will smell water tomorrow. God knows, I could use a nice cool spring."

"I'm absolutely certain that your way is that much better than what I suggested," muttered Macallan under his breath. He might have to share the water as Doc decided, but he still didn't have to like the mouthy little Napoleon.

Exhausted, the men drank their share of water, stacked the saddle from Buck with the gear from the pack horse in one pile. Too tired and thirsty to be hungry, they fed and rubbed the animals down, hobbled them to allow grazing on any close foliage.

"Always wondered why anyone would join the cavalry'" said Holliday.

"Especially knowing they were going to West Texas to fight Indians in the most God forsaken land man has ever lived in. If I was President, I would let them Indians have all of that country they want. Figure if they didn't have to fight for it, they'd probably be damn tired of living there in the cactus and sand and would move to Canada. Might freeze their asses off up there, but at least they could get a drink of water every now and then."

"I didn't know what the land was like when I volunteered. The books all made it sound exciting," said Macallan.

"Welcome to all the parched excitement a man could ever want," said Holliday. "I'll take the first 'exciting' watch. "I know them Kiowas are out there. Let's just take a one hour watch at a time. Mease, you up for standing watch yet?"

"I can handle it if I can sit."

"Sit it is. Everyone keep your weapons at hand and loaded."

Leaning against the pile of gear and facing outward, everyone except Holliday was asleep in seconds. He walked slowly back and forth, listening to the horses and the night. "Johnny," he thought, "You best be watching your back around these three. They don't seem overly concerned about your well being." When his watch ended, he woke English and despite his worries, fell into a deep sleep.

The small band again rose early in the dark, saddled Buck, loaded the pack horse whom they had named Goat, and were moving while the air still carried a chill. Mease rode the travois, with Holliday on Buck, and the other two walked out to the sides of the horses trail. Nothing moved on the mesa except the small birds which peeped when disturbed by the men. Soon the birds were absent and the heat rose as the light became stronger.

Slowly, step by painful step, they trekked onward, fighting the terrible thirst and heat. The animals were showing signs of distress today. Soon their limit would be reached. Doc rechecked the rudimentary map given him by Sheriff Jensen back in Jackboro. It showed a major river less than two days north. He changed the direction of the struggling band to directly north, hoping the hand drawn map was accurate. They needed water desperately.

By early afternoon, Holliday began to feel uneasy. The slight tensing of his shoulders, the constant feeling of being watched, kept him turning to check their trail. His neck had become stiff from looking back so frequently. He was developing a fierce headache. Still unable to see what was following them, by now he was certain they were there. The first few streamers of dust, made him distrust his feelings because they were so quickly dissipated by the breeze. As the dust started building higher, he knew the Indians were following and getting closer. Finally he sang out to the group. "Don't look back and don't pick up speed. We are being tailed. We need to find a defensive position.

"I see a tree, figure it to be bout a mile ahead. Ain't much of a tree but I'm not picking up any other cover right now. There's some low brush near the tree," said English. "If we got more than a half mile lead on those Kiowas, we could make it. They'd catch us if they're closer and we run now. Maybe we oughta wait and see, can we get just a little closer. Seems like as long as we walk, they follow us walking also. I got a feeling that when we start running they are going to kick everything up to a higher speed."

The men all looked at the small tree and low bushes in the undulating heat waves. It seemed poor cover at best but there was nothing that looked better. By the time they made it to the tree, they knew they could be swarmed and overrun by the hostile Indian band.

Macallan turned and watched their trail. A thin thread of dust was all he could see. The gray-white sand was lifted by the heat broken up to hang still in the higher air.

"It looks like they are gaining." Macallan called out. Turning and walking forward, "Probably time we begin a run for that tree."

"Wait, before we go," said Holliday, "Watch ahead and call out if you see hostiles ahead of us. These men are hunters and they could be driving us toward an ambush. Be ready if that brush up there is full of Indians, we gotta take the position anyway so charge them. Now, make sure your weapons are loaded, get a good grip on Buck's tail and he'll help you get more speed. Alright, let's go – all out."

The ragged, tired band forced aching bodies and legs to their utmost. Small cacti and plants they had easily stepped over before now seemed to reach out to grab for tired legs. Fast shallow breaths brought in alkaline dust. Throats, chests and legs burned. Now only one block to go, Macallan tripped, and English grabbed his arm, helping him up. Closing now, they could see the tree stood at an entrance to a break in the mesa's surface, the beginning of an arroyo leading west. There were a few sparse greasewood bushes growing up from the opening in the ground.

Holliday raced to the edge and jumped Buck into the wash, still holding the leads for the pack horse behind him. The horses lurched as their hooves sunk deeply into the loose sand bottom. The travois head dropped rapidly then the rear crashed unevenly, flipping Mease out onto the wash's bottom. Holliday slid off Buck's back. He led both horses deeper into the arroyo tying them securely to a tree. Mease forced himself painfully to his feet and struggled to the edge of the arroyo, near where it was secured by a clump of thin greasewood bushes. Pushing the intense pain of his wound from his mind, he forced himself stomach down against the bank, with his head, arms, and weapon above the edge of the draw. He watched the enemy approach rapidly, braced his Spencer against the mouth of the wash, and shot the lead Kiowa's horse at the base of his throat at seventy yards. The round ripped through the animal's jugular veins, continued on into its lungs. Killing it instantly. It crashed chest down onto the high mesa, throwing the Kiowa at least thirty feet in front of the dead animal. The man crashed hard, rolled several times, then stood, ran to meet another Indian, who offered him an arm. The rider pulled the downed man high into the air. He landed gracefully behind the rider and the two rode off. The shot horse spasmed violently for several seconds and then flipped onto its side and remained motionless.

Holliday had returned to take a position next to Mease. Macallan and English, thrown over the edge when Buck jumped, struggled back to the edge of the arroyo. The four men forming a strong defensive line, began to lay down steady accurate fire, demonstrating their ability to repel a head on attack.

As the Indians turned, Holliday shouted, "Save your ammo, fire only one round at a time, let them get closer if they dare. Could be we can capture several of their horses."

The Kiowas had charged to within fifty yards of the men, but after drawing fire, retired out of rifle range and worked their way back to the east.

"Looks like they are looking to enter the arroyo further down and work their way back up to us," said English. "Anybody get hit?"

The tired group checked for any wounds. Finding none, they moved further into the wash, looking to secure a better defensive line that would not be easily breached by the Kiowas. They found a narrow twist in the arroyo, twenty yards down from the pinion tree, and began walling it up with stones, branches, and sand, building quickly until the wall was five feet high. It wouldn't stand a sustained attack, but it was a barrier of sorts. It would at least slow their attackers down.

"Well," English said, "we are open to attack from all three sides above us and we need to guard the opening. If I was a Kiowa, I would raise a ruckus down here, then send a couple of rifles up to the edge to pick us off. So I'm suggesting we have one man watching each way and have him not get distracted by what's going on elsewhere."

Mease struggled down the wash about half-way to the barrier, laid himself gently against one side of the wash and volunteered, "I'll watch that rim right there. If that's acceptable to y'all."

"I'll take the rim opposite him," said Holliday. English walked over to the barricade and said, "I'll fight right here. I like my killing close up. They'll never get through me."

Macallan sat down by Mease and pointed to the pinion tree, "I got that section covered. If we can hold it till dark, maybe we'll get outta here. It would be sweet to see one more dawn."

One of the Indians stuck his rifle over the barricade and fired. Macallan already prepared had his gun pointed at the barricade, and when the man's head appeared, he pulled the trigger at a distance of less than ten feet. The .50 caliber round entered the man's right eye, exploding blood and a thin viscous liquid out over the barricade. The top of the man's head was torn physically off the lower half. His body was thrown backward, his arm had caught in a tree and was all the men could see of him behind the wall. The bullet from the Indian's rifle hit Holliday. At that close range, the force threw him around and smashed him into the wall of the gully. Opening his shirt, he saw a six inch tear in his skin along his left side where the round had entered, bounced off a rib and exited. The wound, while not serious was painful and bled rather freely.

"Damn, watch close men. They have regrouped fast," he cried and pointed his Winchester at the edge of the gully.

"Anyone get a good count of 'em?" asked MaCalllan. "Looked like ten to fifteen of them to me."

English responded, "At least twelve is what I counted through the heat shimmers. Couldn't see the clearest in that light. I got one, so figure on it to be at least eleven more.

One of the Kiowas fired from the edge down at Lynn and missed, but when the men looked, another two began firing at them from the barricade. English was able to hit one of the two before they retreated again.

"This ain't working," said Holliday. "They getting too close. I'm going out to clear the edge and will be over behind that dead horse. If I can make it out there, that will give you three the barricade. I'll keep them off the edge."

He ran up the side where they had entered, ducked behind the pinion tree and shot a brave standing out on the mesa. Surprised by Holliday's appearance, the man had just stood and watched as Doc seemed to float out of the wash. The bullet from Holliday's Winchester knocked the Indian backward. He crashed into some mesquite and was silent. Doc ran for cover behind the horse. Lying behind it, he could clearly see the rim of the arroyo. No other hostiles were visible near the edge.

The situation for Doc was excellent strategically, but physically was unpleasant. He had an open field of fire which controlled the mesa before him, but his open wound and the heat at this position was rapidly becoming unbearable. The sun blazed down on him while the heat from the mesa floor radiated upward. He searched the horse, found an Indian's water pouch which contained close to a full cup of water. Holliday drank it down greedily.

Placing the water pouch over the horse's penis, he pushed against its bladder to force some liquid out and was rewarded with an addition half cup of liquid. The taste was repulsive, but it was wet. He refocused his attention on the mesa ahead of him and keeping the gully rim free from attack.

Using his knife, he cut a large thick piece of haunch off the dead animal. If he made it back to the group tonight, this would be dinner. Suddenly an arrow landed with a thunk into the ground five feet behind the spot where Holliday sat. He looked around quickly and could see no one. Two more arrows came down before he figured it out. The hunting party was shooting arrows almost straight into the air. The arrows were coming almost straight down. A very difficult shot, but sooner or later, they would be lucky.

The besieged man cut several more long thick chunks of meat from the horse which he used to cover his legs and lower abdomen. He squeezed as far as he could under it lengthwise, then slipped his upper body under the front leg of the horse and with only his head peeking out over the neck of the animal, he was as protected as he could get.

The Indians shot another twenty arrows into the air attempting to hit him. The arrows hit the thick chunks of the horse flesh twice causing the meat to slide off his legs, but causing him no injury .

Watching closely, he saw motion in the brush. Difficult to make out shapes in the deeper brush, mostly he could hear only slight rustling amidst the branches and leaves. Now he picked up several small bushes moving slightly. Time for him to take a maybe shot, he laid the Winchester's sights mid-bush, braced against the horse's neck, and waited. He fought the shimmering heat waves and the sweat running down into his eyes, trying to focus his attention on the one small area. He sucked slowly on small chunks of raw horse meat he had cut earlier to keepa little moisture in his mouth. A bird fluttered near the bushes he was watching. He began to exert pressure on the trigger. The movement, when it became readily visible, seemed unreal in the rising air currents, as a brave rose to loose an arrow. Holliday shot him mid-torso. With the amount of blood exploding from the man's chest, he knew the enemy's numbers were now ten or less.

CHAPTER EIGHT

"Don't know about you two, but I'm getting a craw full of that know-everything bastard. Seems like everything we say or do, Holliday knows better. Truth of it is, we're the damn Cavalry, letting this short stuff ride rough shod over us all. We're the ones should be saying what we do." Macallan was sitting ten feet inside the barricade with his rifle pointed at the opening. He felt it was time to air his displeasure with the heavy handed way Holliday had assumed command of the group. "I say we shoot the skunk. He's got it coming for shooting Bogar."

"I agree with you totally," said Mease. "I know I ain't feeling too sassy right now, but I'll be full of spit within a week. He's a two-bit gambler. We are the Cavalry. We're the ones who know this country. He has no respect at all for us. We would stand a better chance with two horses and only three men."

"There's stuff you both got to puzzle on a little here," said English. "Like, when you gave him your word so he would save our lives. We'd have all three been dead if he hadn't helped with that ambush. And him saving Mouse's life when he took the arrow out. And he knows the way to where we're going and we don't. So what I'm saying here is that I'm Army with you, but I don't think Holliday has done too bad with the trip this far."

"I'm not all that sure we couldn't have fought our way out of there. I know we could have found that campsite. If we hadn't met him, we would be headed back to Texas now. I was glad to have Doc take that arrow out of Mouse, but if we had gone back to Fort Richardson, he would have been treated by an army doctor and been okay now anyway. Well that's what I think, now why don't you think on that. Hell you ain't done no thinking for yourself since we met him. We can talk later, but you just remember what I'm telling you," said Macallan.

"You both gave him your word. What is your word worth," said English.

"You gave your word to Bogar, too, didn't you? Does your word to Holliday mean that much more than your friendship oath to Ham? You need to spend more time thinking on your loyalties," said Macallan.

CHAPTER NINE

The rapid inaccurate enemy count by English had now been lowered to nine men. By the time darkness mercifully came, Doc returned to the arroyo. Halloing the men well back from the lip of the arroyo, he slid into camp. The three welcomed him back. They looked exhausted and seeing the meat, put more wood on the fire. Within minutes, the ravenous men ate the half-cooked horse flesh. Macallan remarked it could easily be the best meal he had ever slid over his tongue. English said, "I don't know why the Kiowas don't fight at night, but we can get some sleep and get ready for the morning. There can't be but nine or ten of them left." Holliday began to saddle up Buck. "You thinking we should ride on tonight and try to slip them?' asked Macallan.

"Nope. I'm tired of being under attack. I know I can't cuddle up with that damn dead horse for one more day. Probably ain't got more than two cups of water left in my body. Figure I'm going out there tonight and kill them sons of bitches. That way maybe we can really sleep tonight and get ready to move peacefully in the morning. Cause, you know what? I got no problem with fighting at night. Truth is, I'd rather die with a gun in my hand than by being slowly cooked by the sun under that rotting dead horse out there."

"I'll come with you," said English.

"Only if you're sure. There's nine or more mean Indians out there and if they take you alive, you'll scream for days."

"I'm coming to help. Like you say, we're dying slow here anyway."

"Check your pistol. Make sure it's loaded and cocked. Leave your rifle here in case they break this way. Macallan and Mease will need it to beat them back. Keep your mouth shut and do what I say. No talking when we leave camp. Now cock that pistol."

"Okay," English pulled out his pistol, checked the loads and cocked it. Macallan shot a glance at Mease, who nodded his head slowly back at him.

CHAPTER TEN

Holliday left the arroyo leading Buck. English followed with a determined look on his face. Twenty yards out, Holliday stopped. "We need to get our eyes accustomed to the dark. When we find them, don't look at the fire. Shoot fast, shoot at movement."

They both rode Buck. English knew they were heading east when they left the arroyo, but within the twenty minute ride, he lost all sense of direction due to the twists and turns Holliday was taking. Soon, they entered the base of a wide gully, which English figured was the downstream wash of the arroyo Mease and Macallan were still in. Sitting behind Holliday, George could see little. Doc began heading up the wide wash slowly. Within minutes, they saw the flicker of the Kiowas fire. They sat on Buck's back while they surveyed the scene. There were five Kiowa's sitting around a small fire, with several sleeping at random around the campsite.

"Keep your gun in your hand. Shoot at any movement you see on the ground. Do not wait, this is not a fair fight, if you don't kill them and kill them fast, they kill you." Holliday put his loaded and cocked Colt .45 into his left hand, then reaching behind him, he pulled his .38 caliber pistol from the holster built into the back of his jacket. He cocked it, looked at English, "Here we go."

English's mouth was far too dry to speak, but he drew his pistol and nodded. His heart was beating so loudly he felt sure the Indians could hear it. He wanted nothing more than to be sitting back in the arroyo with Mease and Macallan. He deeply regretted volunteering with Holliday.Doc, a pistol in each hand, the reins held between his teeth, kicked Buck forward and rode to the center of the Kiowas' camp. He shot into the face of the first Kiowa at a distance of five feet. The four remaining Indians scrambled for their weapons, Doc alternately firing his .38 and .45, shot all four rapidly. Throwing his leg over Buck's neck, he slid to the ground, landed gently on his feet and with both guns held before him, he shot two Indians who had been sleeping and had raised their heads while Doc was walking toward them. He killed both with head shots. He walked slowly about the camp. Holliday was the only thing moving. To English, still sitting on the horse, Holliday's pistols fired so fast that it sounded like one long roar. He kicked the fire, lifting one log into the air. The embers under the log burst into flames, lighting the area more that expected. Doc dodged to one side to avoid the flames, and squinted through the night, trying to find his remaining enemies. A rifle shot brushed his cheek and he threw two rounds at the flash. He opened his Colt .45 and thumbed in new shells. Sensing movement to his right, he dropped to one knee and fired as the last Indian levered a round into his rifle. The man was blasted over backward.

Dropping his empty pistols into their holsters, he pulled the lanyard from around his neck and stabbed each of the Indians deep in their chest. Two tried to evade him, but now all were dead. He began searching for water pouches, found several, threw one to English and drank the contents of the other down. He felt there must have been at least two cups of water in it.

Replacing his knife, he again drew his pistols and reloaded them. Once reheeled, he looked around the camp. "Nine of em, good counting English." George still sat on Buck. He had been motionless throughout the fight. He had been so terrified that he had done nothing at all.

"Uncock that weight in your hand and put it away," said Holliday. "I'm uncomfortable with a ready pistol looking down on me."

"Sorry ," said English, as he released the hammer of the Colt and holstered it. "I was no help at all. I sat there like a damn buffalo chip. I am sorry, sorry I didn't help."

The man's voice struck a chord that resonated deeply within Doc. Some would regard Holliday as a soul-less killer, but he could still feel the sorrow and regret of every death. "You're not the first to freeze up in a close fight." he said. "Somehow close up makes your own death seem more real. You know you're going to get it someday, but today you got it to wait just a little while. Hell, we all got death coming, but it's one of those things no one likes to ponder on too much. Best just let it go. It's always better to feel bad later than to have the other guy feeling bad over you."

"Good thing here, Mr. English, is that I feel I can trust you. I wouldn't have brought Macallan with me; I feel a resentment in him. He's got a dislike of me that goes deep. Trust here is going to be the glue that holds us together or destroys us before we find

83

civilization. I'm looking for you to watch my back, just like I watch yours."

"Now, let's see what we got for horses. We should all be riding now. Keep looking for more water bags too. Don't know how soon till we find water."

In a make-shift corral of branches and rope, stood twelve Indian ponies Working quietly, steadily, the men secured the twelve nervous animals. Leading them out by the campfire, Holliday said, "Take your pick, English. You came for the fight, you get the reward."

They were mostly brown colored with a few pintos. All were unshod. English picked the tallest of the animals. They were all a little spooked with the unfamiliar smell of the white men and the raw coppery smell of the fresh blood of their previous owners.

Fashioning a rope halter, English threw a blanket on his new mustang, and jumped on the horse's back. The animal hunched its back, stood stock still, then began a stiff-legged hop about the area. He kicked it in the ribs, and it started trotting about the fire. When he pulled back, it stopped and stood still wide-eyed with fear looking at Holliday.

"I like him. He's got a little spirit and that's good," said English, throwing his right leg over and sliding off the horse.

"Now let's get the other blankets, and the clothes off the bodies, any knives, guns and ammo we can find, and we'll head back."

"Why are you taking their clothes?" asked English.

"They are dirty now, but we should find the river soon and wash them. We can use them for bandages. The other thing is we gotta get clothes for the three of you. You go into town with those uniforms and it's like shouting that you're deserters. If possible, we should try to keep you from hanging. The horses, knifes, and guns, we can sell and buy better clothes when we hit a town. We might end up having a handy little nest egg."

The two victorious men returned to camp with the spoils of war. The removal of the enemy, the additional horses, and the absolute knowledge that tomorrow would be a much better day for travel, improved the mood of everyone. Holliday pulled out his bottle and each had a victory drink. Then exhausted, he went to a place near the fire and slept almost immediately. English said, "I will take the first watch, you two get some sleep if you can. We couldn't find any more Kiowas, but that don't mean there's none out there."

When they woke Holliday, they had already made coffee, and the three were working hard on building their first smoke. Doc rose slowly, feeling something wasn't quite right. They all seemed very interested in rolling a cigarette. Usually there was some talk. It was the first time he hadn't been up first, and he wasn't happy they were into his stuff. "Whatcha thinking guys?" He said, and all three heard turned quickly to look at him. " More dead horse for breakfast or should we trust to luck and shoot a deer along the way?"

"Let's have horse," said Mease. "I'm feeling distinctly poorly this morning. Another hour of rest would be good for me."

"Mr. English, will you go get some fresh horse steaks for us while I look at Mr. Mease's wound?" asked Holliday.

"Pull that shirt off and let's get a look at it."

85

Mease's right side was swollen and the skin had stretched over the injury until it was a white color. The white was surrounded by ugly, bright red skin. Doc touched the area four inches up from the actual wound and Mease winced.

"You're infected, that damn thing has turned septic. I think I should cut it open and drain it. Get at least some of the poison out and give your body a chance to fight the sepsis. What do you think Macallan, what would you guys do in the Army?"

"The medical corps would have probably put him in bed and waited to see what happened."

"There's your two choices, Mease. Which would you like, we can let you rest today, or I can cut that open and see if that helps."

"Doc, you know a lot more than me about medicine, I'm trusting you to do what you feel best. Cut it, drain it, let me have one more day in the drag sleigh. We need water soon. Can't wait here. Let's do it now so I can have some steak, and we can travel." Mease's words were strong but in his heart he knew he was going to die. He felt too weak to recover so why not get it done quick.

Once again, Holliday took out his scalpel and heated the blade in the fire. "I'm not going to cauterize it this time, because it's spread too far. If I can get some of the sepsis out though, your body may fight back easier. One more thing, Mease, I know this makes you feel weak and you suspect you're going to die. If you don't change that kinda thinking and begin trying to live right now, you will die. The harder you try to live the better your chances to make it."

"Okay Doc, I know you can save me."

DOC HOLLIDAY: THE HARD RIDE

Holliday's blade cut deep and quick. Through the opening, dark brownish liquid rolled out and down Meases's abdomen. Holliday wiped it off with some of the Indian's clothing and gently applied pressure above and below the wound. When the fluids stopped seeping out, Holliday washed the area with whiskey. He left the wound open. He told Mease, "Cover it lightly with your shirt. For the most part, it will heal from within. If this helps, you'll be okay. I've seen worse cases survive. You can too if you try."

The injured man laid back. Too exhausted to move, still he felt he had to eat to regain his strength, and he cut into his horse steak.

After breakfast, the band began packing their supplies on one of the Indian ponies, Holliday saddled Buck, while Macallan and English fashioned rope halters for their ponies. They led the pack horse out first and fastened the travois to its hind quarters. While Holliday sat on Buck to control the animal, they assisted Mease to the travois. Macallan mounted his pony first and it remained calm. Being around the white man smell all night had conditioned it to accept one as a rider. Giving both leads for the string of horses to Macallan, English mounted himself. His pony knotted up his back again and hopped about the campsite on stiff legs. He didn't appear to be trying to unseat the man as much as just warming himself up. After his hardheaded mustang had settled down a little, English took one of the leads from Macallan and rode out of the arroyo. He didn't mind that his horse had an independent streak. He found stubborn horses were better mounts.

Once again Holliday took the lead, he was moving at a faster pace this morning. Mease's comfort was a concern, but getting to water weighed heavily on all their minds. They followed Holliday's compass straight north.

They crossed where the gully had run its course. Traveling over open areas of sand and sage with a sprinkling of granite rocks uncovered by the times the clouds had opened and dumped inches of rain on the hard earth. The water had swept through the small gully and washed any loose soil or sand before it. The land here was changing from the flat alkali mesa to broken land with small hills, rolling ridges with trees and grass. The smoothness of the softer passage allowed the travelers to gain a little speed offset by the longer trail around many of the hillocks and buttes. A gentle wind began to blow in the early afternoon and except for their overpowering thirst, the ride was indeed more comfortable. A small doe broke cover and English harvested it for their evening meal. The men's spirits improved dramatically. Mease suggested that the four band together and start a small ranch where they would be able to run a few beefs. With hard work, they could make a success here where land was available. Macallan thought a general store would be more of a money making endeavor since they knew little about ranching. English was of a mind that livery and blacksmithing would always be needed as the land grew. Holliday kept his own counsel, but knew there'd be no going into business with these men.

The three men agreed that they should be able to sell the horses and goods taken from the Indians for a good nest egg, maybe even up to as much as 500 dollars. New clothes and better mounts were the two agreed upon new purchases. As the sun began to paint the ground a light purple, they came to a large river.

"Must be the Columbia," said Holliday. "It's the only one I saw on the map that could be this large." Without hesitation they headed the horses out into the river, far enough that they could stand and drink deeply. They slid off their horses, helped Mease out of the travois, and luxuriated in the overpowering wetness they had so desperately craved.

Holliday collected the canteens, and waded out into the river where it wasn't muddied by the horses and the men. He was bending over, filling them when a force hit him, low in the back, throwing him forward into the deeper stream of the river. Unconscious, he floated away downstream face down.

The Spencer's roar, so close, spooked the half-wild horses. They jerked hard on the leads, pulling Mease and English off their feet, landing them face deep in the water as they struggled to hold tight to the pitching animals. English was first to recover his feet. He stood with his pistol already pulled and prepared to return fire to whoever was attacking them. He was shocked to see Macallan standing still, the smoking rifle in his hands, aimed at the floating body of Holliday. Still startled from the shot, English's eyes searched the shore for hostile, but soon came to realize it had to be Macallan who had shot Holliday. English lowered his pistol until it was aimed at the trooper's head. "Lower that rifle."

"What, you figuring on shooting me, English?"

English held his pistol rock solid on Macallan's head at a distance of less than six feet. "I'm thinking hard on it, Irish. You don't lower that rifle, you will soon be floating with Holliday. You just proved to me you can't be trusted. I never imagined you to be a back-shooting skunk."

Macallan didn't even look over at English. He lowered his rifle, and watched Holliday's body float around the bend in the river. Turning with a smile, he said, "Damn nice not having that overbearing bastard around." He went back to Buck, pulled Holliday's gear off the animals and began moving his stuff from the Indian pony he had been riding to Buck. He rifled through Holliday's gear, taking his whiskey, tobacco, a small poke of cash, then spread his extra clothes on the ground. "Anyone want anything?" he asked.

"Put the pistol away, English. Put it away or use it, you're starting to irritate me. You know you can trust me, George, how long we been together?" Macallan was showing his friendly smiling face. "You knew I hated being rode over rough shod by that cantankerous little bastard. How many times have I said we gotta get rid of him. We're rid of him now, we better off now too is the way I see it."

"You would see it that way, you sniveling weasel. I swear, you're lower than the track of a snake's belly. Do you have a compass? Do you have the canteens? Got any idea which way we go? You're a stupid, greedy backshooter, and if we didn't need you, by God, I would shoot you right here," said English.

"Put the gun away, George," said Mease moving over to stand by Macallan. "It's been us three since the beginning and it will be us

90

three that end this. Now get your crap together, and let's move before we're landed on by some passing bunch of Indians."

CHAPTER ELEVEN

Doc regained consciousness floating face down in the water. He struggled to get his head up for a big drink of fresh air. He rolled in the water to be on his back and get his face up. He couldn't get his legs to work but by using his arms, he finally managed the maneuver. His left arm was still weighted down by the canteens. He pulled them up, emptied the water out. and tied the now bouyant canteens behind his head and neck making it easier for him to keep his mouth and nose above water. He looked around seeing nothing but river and wild shoreline. What happened? He remembered only walking into the water to fill the canteens. Now he was floating down a river with no one around.

His legs refused to move. Checking them further, he found they were numb. To be hit that suddenly, he figured there must have been a hostile Indian party hidden in the trees by the site where he and the cavalrymen had led their horses into the water. So, the three Cavalry men were probably now dead. He was utterly alone, helpless. No horse, no grub, no people, that he knew of within five hundred miles. His thoughts were disrupted by his hand touching something solid. He grabbed at it. It was a half-submerged tree still rooted on the shore but washed so much of it was leaning down into the water. Easing his body alongside the branch, he began skulling himself shoreward with one hand while he paddled with the other. Pulling his body half over a large branch, he rested. "As long as you're still alive," he thought, "Johnnie, you still got a chance to get through this." He began taking inventory. His colt .45 was still in his holster held by the leather thumb strap. Loaded, that meant he had at least six rounds for protection. He could feel another sixteen rounds in the holster belt. His knife was still hanging around his neck by the lanyard.

He reached for his .38 caliber pistol but found when his hand reached behind him, the gun was smashed beyond repair. He dropped it in the river. There was blood on his hand when he brought it in front of him. The bullet that hit him must have been stopped by the pistol or he would have been killed. The blow to his lower back left him with no feeling in or use of his legs. Struggling to feel down his leg to his boot, he found himself unable to reach far enough to know whether he still had his derringer. Looking at the tree body, he doubted he would be able to force his body through the heavy limbs. He slid over the branch into the leeward current and kept pulling himself along the branch while using his other arm to push against the bottom. The water was less than a foot deep here, but he was still ten yards to shore. The coldness of the water and the cool breeze blowing on his wet clothes were weakening him further.

Finally, abandoning the tree branch, he used his arms to reach down and push himself toward shore. At the rivers bank, he used exposed roots and grass to pull himself free from the water. Using a driftwood branch, he tried to force himself to stand. He found he was regaining partial feeling in his left leg. "You can do this, John," he said, pushing himself erect with his left leg. He found he could stand on both legs, but his right leg was completely out of his control for walking. Using the branch as his right leg, and hopping short distances with his left leg, he worked his way up the bank, away from the river.

He camped cold that night, shivering alone in the dark, with the cool air, a gentle breeze, and wet clothes. By early morning, he'd regained some strength and continued hobbling forward searching for a place he could use as a shelter. He needed protection from the elements where he could build a fire and begin working on regaining the full use of his legs.

By mid morning, he stumbled across a rough one room shack, breathed a sigh of relief, maybe he would be able to survive this after all.

The place had been abandoned for quite a long time. Dirt and dust lay thick on everything but there was at least a rudimentary fireplace built into one wall, and a bed nailed into the opposite wall. He knocked the dust off the cot with his crutch, and threw a few chunks of wood into the fireplace, from the stack leaning against one wall, Using the flint sitting on the hearth, he lit a fire and then sat on the cot. 'Long day' was his last thought as he lapsed into unconsciousness again.

At mid-morning of the next day, he was awakened by the thunder of horse's hooves pounding up to the door. He forced himself up, hobbled to the door, refastened his holster belt and gun back onto his hip, and hopped out of the door using his crutch. He was surrounded by a group of Comanche's . Realizing he had no possibility of coming out of this alive, he dropped his crutch, unfastened his leather hammer lock from his gun prepared to fight to the death. Intentions aside, he fell forward onto his face, unconscious. His last though before hitting the ground was, "I hope they kill me fast."

CHAPTER TWELVE

The three cavalrymen stayed by the river that day. They washed the clothing taken from the Indians. Trying to disguise their uniforms, they changed into three passable shirts. Boots, trousers, and hats were all still Army. It was a long day for English wrestling with his morals while dealing with the day's events. Macallan and Mease were his friends. He couldn't abandon them, yet his conscience ate at him. His friends had given their word and still just shot Holliday in the back. A simple honest man who had joined the Army to serve his country, now, because of his faith in his friends, he was a traitor, a murderer, and a thief. "Why," he thought, "Did I ever cross that river. I should have stayed with the patrol and returned to the Fort. I listened to Macallan when I should have used the little horse sense I have." He had rapidly moved from trooper to outlaw with a rope waiting. There was no escape at this point, he had to ride this string until he could separate himself from Mease and Macallan or until its end. At some point he might break free from them, set up somewhere on his own, but for now, he was forced to play the hand he was dealt.

On the other side of the coin, Macallan was feeling quite pleased with the turn of events. He had hated Holliday and was glad to be shed of him. Now he had fulfilled his vow of vengeance for Bogar.

DOC HOLLIDAY: THE HARD RIDE

He'd killed the little bastard, Holliday, and in this case, any way to kill was good. He had taken over as leader.

Things were going to be done his way. The three would ride on together. English was going to be a pain and needed watching, but Mease was with him. English would come around or be left behind.

The next morning they started again for Denver. Macallan took Buck; Mease and English rode Indian ponies and with the remuda in tow, the three started straight north. The travel was faster and much easier with the horses. Water was no longer the overpowering need as they ran across several smaller creeks and rivers as they rode.

They saw no trace of Indians. The rain started on the afternoon of the first day. A gentle sprinkle cut the heat and at first helped them , but it gradually built to a heavy rain, and by evening they were soaked through with no real hope for a fire. They sat in the rain, cold, miserable, and hungry.

They started early again. The rain had stopped during the night. Still wet and shivering in the low early morning temperature, the Army men kept a fast pace through the rough country, circling the many short bluffs and hills, trying always to keep to the straightest course north. By early afternoon, the rough hills, smoothed themselves into long rolling hills with gentle green valleys. Few gully's or hills remained. This was the land beaten smooth by countless years of buffalo herds. Visibility seemed unlimited and riding was easy.

Mease was suffering with the pain from his wound. The pony was a rough ride. Barely broken, he had a rough gait. The continual bouncing irritated the wound. Yesterday's rain followed by last night's cold had depleted Mease's energy. His wound when he examined it, looked good. He pulled his horse up stopping the group.

"What?" said Macallan, reining in Buck.

"I want the good horse," said Mease. "This pony rides rough. The pain is too intense. I want the better horse. I need a smoother ride."

"Get off him and walk if he is that bad."

"You best stop your mouth and start using your brain. You do not talk to me that way. You may have duped Holliday, you'll not deceive me. Now get off that horse and keep your mouth shut. If I'm going to die from riding a half-broke horse, Macallan, you will be there holding my hand when we cross the river into hell." Mease unbuttoned his holster, "So I will say it one last time. Switch horses with me."

Macallan slid from Buck's saddle and led him over to Mease. "Christ, you getting damn feisty here lately. Take it the fuck easy."

"Ever since you bushwhacked Holliday, you been thinking you're the big dog. You can forget that crap now. You gotta be a helluva lot tougher than you to buffalo me and George. You better decide you're one of us. Remember what happened to the last turd that thought he was boss?"

Macallan knew better than to front Mease. Injured and sick he might be today, a formidable foe he would always be. Macallan sadly watched as his leadership of the three disappear with Mease's challenge.   "Still," he thought, "Better to be tight with a group of three friends, than alone and in charge of nothing."

That night, they had a fire and fresh meat. Three days later they rode into a small town named Alapine Springs.

CHAPTER THIRTEEN

The lanterns were burning late at The Saloon. The larger of the two bars in town, The Saloon had two stories. It had been built in earlier times before the mining ran dry, and the bar still had working girls. Four months earlier, the three ex-cavalrymen had sold their string of horses for a half share in The Saloon and the Mercantile. Indian-broke ponies brought a premium from the local cowboys, and they had done much better than they expected. Macallan and Mease worked at the bar, while English handled the General Store. The men remained close friends and had agreed to share all profits equally. Thus far they had succeeded beyond greediest dreams.

Tonight's poker game had started early. Macallan's luck was still running hot and he had been quite a bit ahead by the time most cowboys and locals had thrown in their hand and gone home. Macallan, Mease, and English continued playing on into the night with Old Lake Blasick, half-owner of The Saloon. It had not been a good night for Blasick and the majority of funds used in the game sat before Macallan.

Macallan had been playing aggressively all night. His current hand held two pair, kings and tens, and he was betting it heavily. Blasick, already down a thousand dollars, pulled out his bill carrier and unzipped it. "I figure you to be bluffing Irish. I got another thousand right here says I got the best hand." He pulled a handful of bills out and counted them into the pot. To call would cost Macallan the rest of his previous winnings. Irish pushed all his funds in, "I call."

Blasick turned over his hand. Three sevens. Disgusted, Macallan threw his hand into the middle. "You one lucky sumbitch tonight. That's all for me tonight." He stood and walked over to the bar. "Anyone else want a night-cap?"

He poured out four shots, carried one over to Blasik, and Mease. Then walked back to the bar for the last two. When he turned, his gun was in his hand. Blasik was looking to his left, talking to English, he couldn't see Macallan walk up behind him with his gun drawn. Macallan pulled the trigger, blasting a hole through the back of Blasick's head. "Looks like we are the full owners of the bar now, Boys." He holstered his gun.

"Christ," shouted English, "Are you crazy?

"Shut up," said Macallan. "Look around. We are the only people up in this three horse town. Lynn, get some of Blasick's paper out of the safe. You're going to write a Bill of Sale for The Saloon from Old Lake to you and me. Just copy his name on the bottom of the letter. George, go get his horse. We'll load his body on it and take him out of town about ten miles. Then let his horse just go. Coyotes, buzzards and wolves will chew on his body long enough that no one will ever recognize him. If they do find him, they'll think the old coot had a heart attack on the way out of town."

Mease quickly went to the safe and went to work. He was comfortable now with his new life as a thief and murderer. English was still struggling with the moral dilemma. His life had changed so rapidly that the violence still repelled him. However, he knew there was no going back. He went to get his horse, while Macallan began to clean the bloody mess off the bar room floor.

The next morning, Macallan recorded the deed at the Courthouse. No one questioned him when he said Blasik had lost the bar at poker and decided to leave town right away. Hell, no one ever liked that cheap ornery goat, Old Lake Blasik, anyway.

CHAPTER FOURTEEN

When he regained consciousness, he found he was strung out on the open ground, face down. His arms and legs were each bound separately spread-eagling him. He was totally helpless. Twisting his head, he watched an elderly squaw walk slowly at him. She carried a buffalo robe, brandished a knife, still smoking from the fire's heat. She spread the robe on the ground next to the bound man, kneeling on the robe, she leaned over him. Doc pulled once strongly against the bindings, leather straps, unyielding, probably soaked in water. An older Army scout had described this torture to him while Doc was still in Dallas. He had said that when the leather dried, it would shrink, exerting tremendous pressure on his hands and arms. They would be slowly pulled from his body, although he would probably not be alive to see the second limb rendered from his body. Fear filled him as he remembered the scout's stories of the atrocities the Comanche's had inflicted on their prisoners.

He wished only now to remain brave for the next two hours. Whatever pain she could inflict, he would not pull away. He would not scream. He was a Holliday. He could face pain and death as strongly as anyone. His resolve held firm as the crone sat on the robe next to him. Her knife entered where the flesh near his wounds was beginning to rot. He screamed, jerked once against the bindings and lost unconsciousness. When he recovered his senses, he was wrapped tightly into the robe, the squaw had been sitting on. He was still lying on his stomach, but his bindings had been removed. A large Indian man wearing leather leggings, a breach cloth and with skin turned deep bronze by the sun, was standing next to him.

He stood over Doc, looking down at him, for long minutes. Then he squatted from the knees. For several minutes longer, he sat on his heels, his butt barely two inches from the ground. "You okay to talk?" the man asked Doc.

"Yes, I can talk."

"My name is Sitting Hawk. What is your name?"

"John Holliday, Doctor John Holliday."

"Well, John Holliday, Nashawn say you live. She removed four pieces of iron from your back."

Doc was quiet for several minutes. "She saved my life?"

"Yes. You had four wounds. You would have died soon."

"Seems funny, first you shoot me, then you help me recover."

"Comanche no shoot you. Comanche are brave fighters. They will attack and kill you, but Comanche not back shooter."

"You mean it wasn't the Comanche's that attacked us?"

"Indian not attack when you were injured."

"Well somebody shot me."

"Umm," he grunted. "White hair white eyes shoot you."

"We only had one guy with blonde hair, Macallan. He must have been the guy who shot me."

"Sitting Hawk watch from hill." He was silent looking at Doc. "Comanche surprised to see you alive. White hair not good at killing people."

"Those miserable two-faced Cavalry cowards back shot me."

"Sitting Hawk see their trail heading between the two suns early this morning. They ride fast. Like wolf follow. Maybe you wolf."

"You let them pass?"

"Yes, they are now in the land of the Ute. We have peace with Ute."

Doc's head was whirling. "You speak good English."

"Sitting Hawk scout for Army, two years. Army Colonel paid Indians knowledge, but didn't believe what we told him. Soon scouts don't scout, only make stories for him. Then we quit. No more scouting."

"Them Army dolts don't much listen to anyone."

"Nashawn come. Time to eat. Talk later. Eat and rest."

Doc watched Sitting Hawk's wife walk toward him and wondered how he could have been so wrong about her appearance. Now looking at her he realized she was still in her twenties with a lithe figure. She handed Doc a wooden bowl filled with succulent chunks of meat and what looked to be grass and weeds. He didn't care what the stew was made of , he could have eaten the bowl itself he was so hungry. He thanked her for helping him, but she ignored him other than to give him the food. Together they left the campsite after giving him his food.

Later when Sitting Hawk returned, Doc asked, "Why did you save me? I thought you would kill me back at the shack."

"You very brave. Sitting Hawk sees a bright fire that burns within. You had one gun, stand one leg. You still came out to fight. Tall Elk wanted your hair for power token, but Sitting Hawk wanted teacher."

"I will teach you anything I can."

"I warn you, Tall Elk still wants your hair. Do not trust him."

"If you return my knife and gun, I will not worry about anyone."

Sitting Hawk walked away slowly. Soon he came back with Doc's holster belt. He put Doc's knife on top of the holster.

"I will bring guns when you can teach. I wish to learn to use small gun for fight also. I know rifle, but puzzled by hand gun. Will you teach hand gun?"

"Ain't much too it. Stand close, be fast. That will get you through almost anything. But my answer is yes, if you will wait until tomorrow. I will be stronger tomorrow and I will begin to teach you to fight with a handgun."

"Okay, start tomorrow. Sitting Hawk cannot leave weapon with white man. Too close to women and children."

Early, right after first light, Sitting Hawk came to Doc's campsite. He squatted back on his heels and silently watched the sleeping white man. After several minutes, he cleared his throat softly. No movement from Doc. He coughed a little louder . Doc began to move a little, then turned and looked at Sitting Hawk. "Think there's enough light to shoot by?" he asked."Yes. Hawk known for good eyesight."

"That was a joke," said Doc.

"Yes, I know. I have heard many white man jokes but always fail to see why they waste time telling them. Sitting Hawk's joke funny."

"I can't much tell you, myself," said Doc, climbing out of his robe. He took some time standing. His legs had regained feeling but still felt weak. His back and arms were very stiff. His body's overwork in surviving the river and the surgery was manifested in sore muscles. Sitting Hawk had brought Doc's gun, an additional gun and holster. and an additional Brave who sat a short distance away with a rifle. Doc put on his holster and slipped the gun into it. He worked it in and out several times, checked the loads, seeming to reacquaint himself with the feel. Sitting Hawk also put on a holster and slipped a six-shooter into it.

"Do not make threatening gesture at Sitting Hawk, Moiseia may misunderstand and shoot you."

It was Doc's first look at the Comanche's camp. There were roughly twenty teepees, thrown around in a circle leaving a large open area with a fire pit in the middle. He did not see many people, but there were six or eight younger kids running around and several women working at skins or animals. At first glance, Doc thought what an intelligent, pleasant way to set up a village. His own small campsite was thirty yards away from the Comanche's common area.

Doc led the way, outside of the camp, walking until he came to a dead tree, near the small creek, another thirty yards away from the village. The slow walk helped his muscles loosen up. He stopped twenty feet from the splintered trunk. "Can you hit that stump, Sitting Hawk?"

With pistol raised, aimed at the end of an outstretched arm, Sitting Hawk, squeezed off one round. He grazed the bark on one side of the tree. Immediately all action stopped in the small village, and the children began running down to Sitting Hawk and Doc. Sitting Hawk motioned the children off to one side and had them sit to watch.

"Shoot the last five rounds fast, watch to see where you hit on the tree. Keep moving your gun just a little each time, until you hit the tree in the middle."

Sitting Hawk brought the line of fire in rapidly and drilled the last three rounds dead center on the tree.

"Okay," said Doc. "Time for the first rule of hand guns. Never put in six cartridges. Leave one cylinder empty and keep the hammer on the empty slot to prevent a accidental firing. Rule two of gun fighting, never shoot the fifth round unless your life depends on it. Nothing is more useless than an empty gun. Do you understand?"

"Yes I understand. Just as I would never throw my last knife, never shoot the last bullet."

"Third rule, unlike a rifle, a handgun is extremely inaccurate. That pistol you are using will have a spread of three to four inches at twenty feet." Doc indicated the spread with his hands. "That means that at forty feet, even if you are aimed dead center on your enemy when you pull the trigger, you could miss him on either side because the spread will be at least eight inches. A handgun is good for fighting up close, not at a distance."

"I understand," said Sitting Hawk, "Get as close to the enemy as possible."

"The Fourth rule is that speed is essential. When you are close, you must be first to shoot. Your opponent will be accurate at fifteen feet also."

"Keep ammo in gun, get close for accuracy, be fast."

"Yep, I think you got it. I see you wear your gun on your right leg. Most people do. Now watch my technique at drawing my gun. Tell your man that it is okay for me to shoot my gun. I will only point it away from you. Sitting Hawk raised his hand as a signal to the seated man. Doc said, "This is my own style and the reason I am more accurate than other men." Doc moved his gun holster over to the middle of his belt, with the gun held at belt level slightly to the left side of his body. He held his hand at belt level, six inches from the gun. "This is my draw, I will go through it slowly this time." Doc moved his right hand toward the gun, his thumb landed on the hammer first and as his little and ring finger gripped the butt of the weapon, he pulled the weapon toward his right side just enough for the barrel to clear the holster, he had cocked the hammer all the way, by the time the weapon was clear, the barrel was swinging toward the tree and he fired, using his left hand to recock the hammer. He fired five rounds at the tree, keeping all five bullets within a three inch diameter.

"Did you see how I did that?"

"Yes, I can do this draw with practice."

Doc reloaded. "Would you like to see my draw as it really is?"

"Yes."

Sitting Hawk saw little but a blur that made five holes appear in the trunk.

"Do you have any questions?"

"Why do you not draw from leg like others?"

"I am faster my way," said Doc. "I also started with my holster tied to my leg. Soon I found that my arm ached after several hours of practice. By moving my holster to my belt to hold my gun at mid-body, my arm was in a more natural position. The muscles used to hold my arm farther back on my shoulder, could now be used to assist in the draw and I could practice longer. An additional benefit is that I can relax my chest muscles completely. The more relaxed you can keep your chest muscles, the less resistance your drawing arm has to use to oppose them. Sounds small, but a small amount of increased speed, pays off big.

"Can I draw from the leg?"

"Certainly, Sitting Hawk. Since you are my friend, I try to show you the best way. You can use any method you want to."

They both reloaded their gun.

"Try this, hold your gun at your waist, mid body. Shoot from there. Remember, only five rounds."

He fired five rounds rapidly, landing all five within the main body of the tree.

"Now, hold the pistol at the same height and hold it over at your right side and fire five more rounds."

Sitting Hawk hit the tree only three times aiming from that position.

"That's my lesson for the day," said Doc. "You need to work on your speed of draw and accuracy of shooting, but that all requires little except time and patience. Tomorrow, if you wish, I will teach you the rest of it. I am very tired. Can I rest now?" Once the shooting was obviously finished the children ran back up to the tribal area. Sitting Hawk took Doc's gun and set it to the side with his. The watching Brave returned to the camp.

"Nashawn bring food soon."

"Nashawn is a very good cook. Her food is wonderful."

"I know. Yesterday was raccoon stew. She make good."

"You are lucky to have a wife that is a good cook."

"Nashawn is not married. She is my daughter. In a war party against the Arapahos several years ago, an empty horse was brought back to Nashawn. She moved back to her father's teepee. Her father's teepee was missing the person who ran it. Soon I think she will remarry. Her period of mourning has passed. When she chooses new mate, Sitting Hawk will also be forced to choose mate. Six women are friendly toward Sitting Hawk. All expect him to choose them to care for his teepee. "

Holliday noticed that Sitting Hawk carefully avoided naming people who had been killed, or even that they had been killed. When he asked Sitting Hawk, he took time to phrase his question. "When a warrior is no longer here and will not return to his teepee, why do you no longer mention him or say his name?"

"To name them or talk about those who have traveled to another world could call their spirits back from the land where they are now. We believe the land they have traveled to, to be a better place," said Sitting Hawk. "The unsettled spirits would then remain around the living, while they would mourn for the land they were brought back from."

Nashawn arrived with a bowl of much the same stew as the day before. Today, the two men ate together. Nashawn sat with them but did not eat. Sitting Hawk belched loudly after he finished eating.

"Good manner," said Sitting Hawk quietly to Doc.

Doc belched loudly also. Nashawn smiled broadly and collected the bowls from the men.

"She likes you. You told her she is good cook."

During the third week of Doc's recovery, Sitting Hawk ended their morning walk by the creek, next to where his teepee stood.

He looked at Doc, "Man should sleep inside."

The nights had been cool. A misty rain fell one night. Also, a coyote had been coming closer every night. This morning when he woke, it had been sniffing his feet. Not that he thought the animal would attack, but there were wolves in the area. Sitting Hawk still took his gun after every practice, but the man no longer watched them with his rifle ready.

"Ya, I been thinking I should ask you if I can moving back to the shack where you found me."

Sitting Hawk opened the flap for Doc. "My teepee has only Nashawn and Sitting Hawk. I would welcome you. You may return to the shack if you wish, but my teepee would be more comfortable."

Doc moved his robes into Sitting Hawk's teepee. His guns were sitting in the teepee, but Sitting Hawk obviously did not want Doc wearing them amongst his people. For three more weeks, Doc gradually recovered. His days were much the same. He went for walks, and he worked with Sitting Hawk and his fast draw. Now, he was taken on hunting trips with groups of men from the tribe. He was friendly with several Braves. Their ability to shoot and ride impressed him greatly. Gradually he came to love his life here. The slow friendly pace of life. His breathing was getting better every day with the climate, fresh air, no smoking and no alcohol. His cough had subsided. The living with Sitting Hawk and Nashawn was very enjoyable, although he could feel the tension mounting between him and Nashawn. Sitting Hawk had noticeably moved his robes between the two.

Doc was impressed by the care Sitting Hawk had taken to find a perfect place to set up their village. It was an isolated secretive location high in amongst rugged hills. A small stream ran near their village site, a pass to the east connected them to the wide hunting plateaus, abounding with game. Every avenue of approach was readily observed by scouts. There was plenty of room for the families. Younger tribe members spent time playing and practicing their marksmanship with bows. This was the perfect place to easily conceal and protect twenty to fifty people.

Sitting Hawk joined him one morning for a walk, and each of the men spent the morning enjoying the companionship of the other.

When they returned to Sitting Hawk's teepee, he turned to Doc. In a somber tone, he said, "John, I will be visiting my women friends this evening."

'Strange thing to say to me,' thought Doc. However when the evening meal came, Sitting Hawk was missing. Nashawn served Doc. Then she also vanished. He sat outside the teepee and enjoyed the evening. When full darkness fell, he wrapped himself up in his robes and went to sleep. He was awakened by a slight giggle. He sensed her presence close to him, her hand gently touching his beneath the buffalo robe. The hair on his arms seemed alive to her touch. She slid under the robes, moving her body next to his in a soft embrace. He became alive as never before. Slowly he shifted his body to make room for her. He turned toward her with his right hand reaching slowly in the dark. He pulled her to him. She lowered her face into his chest as she sighed. He felt lightheaded. The palms of his hands and the soles of his feet tingled. He found her nipples were already fully extended. Something deep inside him relaxed and he gave himself totally to the moment. Her hair felt thick and lustrous, smelling clean and very sensual.

His sexual encounters prior to Nashawn had been only of the most basic type. Now he lay with an adult emotionally stable woman who wanted to share her body with him.

The long month, since he had begun the ride, had its effect also. As had her months without a mate. Their first conjoining fevered and only lasted for a short time. He worried that he had disappointed her. Doc, fearless in battle, was saddled with the standard masculine sexual fears. Tonight, for the first time, he wanted to please his partner and not just himself. When her breathing had slowed, he began to speak softly, telling her of her beauty and grace, knowing she wouldn't understand what he was saying, but wanting to say it to her anyway. He began slowly to caress Nashawn's arms and face. He couldn't clearly see her face but knew her beauty and the lustrous quality of her hair. He moved back the robes and by the faint glow of the fire, he saw her full breasts, nipples erect, and began to touch them. Slowly, this time he tasted and stroked. Finally moving his body over hers, he entered her and together they began the slow magical dance of love. Later, holding her close to him, she whispered, "Chahan."

"John, call me John, Nashawn."

By morning, Nashawn was wrapped and sleeping in her own robes. She smiled shyly at Doc as she rose to begin fixing breakfast.

The night had been astounding to Doc. Nashawn was a true sexual woman in a society which accepted women as equals. She had wanted to have sex with him and clearly had enjoyed it. He had slept with his fourteen year old girlfriend back in Georgia. She was gorgeous but too young to understand sensuality. That encounter had been fast, secretive, and very unfulfilling. He had sexual encounters with several of the whores who worked the bars, including Kate, but those experiences were also fast and of a physical nature only. The women usually had a bad body odor as they bathed infrequently. They used bottles of cheap perfume, quick and convenient. Nashawn had bathed, she smelled wonderful. Clearly she had a deep affection for Doc. It had been

115

simply put, the best night of his life. Sex coupled with affection deeply improved the essence of the encounter. Sitting Hawk was outside the teepee, waiting for Doc to arise, and for Nashawn to make breakfast.

"My friends were lonesome. Sorry I could not return to my teepee earlier."

Doc put his hand on Sitting Hawk's shoulder, touching him for the first time.

"Sitting Hawk, you are my friend. I do not wish to take advantage of your friendship. I must tell you, I wish to have my own teepee and to have Nashawn come with me as my life's partner. You are an honorable man and a warrior. I want you to understand that I am also a warrior, but not an honorable man. When you fight, you stand tall and fight bravely. When I fight, I fight to survive. I use whatever I can to survive."

"Each man, each weapon, each battle, demands its own honor. Because you do not fight as I do does not defeat your spirit." Sitting Hawk watched as Doc struggled to understand. Clearly Doc was raised in a society with more rigid rules of bravery and combat than the rules for the Comanche's. Doc grew up in Georgia during the Civil War. A brave man, an honorable man stood in a line with other soldiers and marched across a field toward almost certain death. The enemy casually shot many men down. The heroes of Doc's childhood were those men who returned from the war. Sitting Hawk fought to protect tribe, family, and self. Staying alive was a priority. Bravery and strength were a must.

"I find that life with the Comanche is a wonderful life. Do the Comanche ever accept others to live with them? I would wish if possible to live with the Comanche, but I do not wish to deceive my friend. I have a disease of the lungs. I will die soon. I love the Comanche and would choose to live here for those days I have left. If I could be accepted with your people, your friends would be my friends, your enemies would be my enemies."

"Nashawn has already told me of your disease. Does it bother you now?"

"No, I have felt wonderful since I have come here. The climate has been good for me."

"Yes, the climate and Nashawn."

"What do you mean, Sitting Hawk?"

"I don't have twigs and weeds in my stew. Nashawn is treating your breathing disease. She began treating you the second day you were here."

Doc was lost deep in thought for several minutes. "I am asking you for permission to talk to Nashawn about marriage. I would also like to join your tribe. If I am accepted by the Comanche, I would live here forever."

"You would be a lucky man if she accepts you. I agree, my daughter would be an excellent person to share a teepee with, but she is an adult woman and does not need my permission to marry. John, she is our medicine woman. She will never leave this tribe. If she accepts you, you would have to stay with this tribe."

"I have to tell you also, that I have killed more than twenty men already. White men and Kiowas"

"Do you think I would find fault with you for killing white men and Kiowas? I am Comanche warrior. I have also killed many. I call you friend. First White Man, I call friend. I think Nashawn would be happy with you to share her teepee. I have learned much from you. You would be a valuable member of the tribe, as a hunter and warrior. Come to meeting tonight, sit by my side. I will talk to the tribe."

"I will be honored to sit next to you."

"Anyone may challenge you. If you are challenged, you may be killed. If you win the challenge, friends of the defeated man may attack you. This is a dangerous course for you to take."

"I still accept. I wish to join the Comanche if I may. I have found more happiness and life in several months with the Comanche than I did in thirty years with my own people. I will make a good fighter and hunter for the Comanche. My loyalty, my world, would be Comanche."

Doc walked back down to the creek to bathe. He brushed and washed at his clothes to make them as presentable as possible. He sat alone at his campsite until Nashawn came to take him to the meeting. She walked slowly and with great beauty.

"Nashawn, I love you. You are the most beautiful woman I have ever seen and I wish to share my life with you. Just talking to you give me joy." She led him in, showing him where to sit next to Sitting Hawk. There was a debate raging around the large bonfire. He was pointed at frequently. Sitting Hawk spoke softly to Nashawn, and she departed quietly. Sitting Hawk stood and spoke slowly, looking at each Warrior seated around the fire. When he sat, there was silence. Apparently they had brought a problem to Sitting Hawk and he made a decision. There was an obvious respect for Sitting Hawk.

The women began bringing food to the seated warriors. Nashawn served Sitting Hawk first. "They were demanding that you be removed from the circle. I have named you friend. No one wished to challenge me. Someone may yet challenge you. I have told them you wish to become Comanche, they are talking about that between themselves. If they accept you, you will be put to a test. They agree that if you are accepted, you will have to undergo the Skin Ceremony. The most sacred of our ceremonies is a demonstration of strength and ability to accept pain. Buffalo bones are pushed through the skin and muscle of your chest. They are bound to leather straps and you are lifted in the air. Your hands are free, but you cannot touch the leather straps or buffalo bones or you will have failed. You begin this test at evening. You are accepted or rejected in the morning. They have not agreed that you should be accepted. They may talk until the sun breaks. This may be as painful as the Ceremony, I am sorry."

"I'm watching."

Nashawn returned with a bowl for Doc. She knelt before him, looked upwards to his face and said, "John."

An angry shout was heard from the Brave Doc had come to recognize as Tall Elk. He stood, then walked across the clearing to Doc. Nashawn tried to stand in his way preventing Tall Elk from reaching Doc, but he pushed the woman to the ground an tried to remove Nashawn's bowl from his hands. Doc's grip was iron. The man could not pull the bowl to him. Doc twisted the bowl, released it several inches, then jerked it free from the man's hands. With his grip suddenly knocked free, the man stumbled backward and fell into the dirt. Several laughs and light banter circled the fire. The man jumped to his feet, pulled out a knife, and assumed a fighting stance.

Sitting Hawk stood between the two men, facing a sitting Doc. "This is Tall Elk, he has put his life on the line to keep you from becoming a member of our tribe. He still wants your hair. He also does not want Nashawn to serve you. Now you have embarrassed him before the Tribe, I cannot stop the fight that is coming. He has challenged you to a knife duel. Only one of you can be alive when the fight ends."

Doc stood slowly. He took out his knife, while watching the gesturing Tall Elk. The Brave was working himself into a frenzy, demonstrating his stabs and thrusts to the circle of men. He was shouting at Doc, apparently telling him what pain and humiliation he would inflict on him.

The seated men quickly stood and their robes were quickly cleared by the women of the tribe. Soon Doc and Tall Elk found themselves surrounded by noisy men. Tall Elk rushed at Doc with his knife held shoulder high. He made a downward thrust, swept his knife to the left, then quickly reversed direction and slashed upward, but Doc had jumped to one side avoiding his attack completely. Tall Elk came slowly this time, holding his knife at waist height and swinging it from side to side. Doc shrunk back toward the circle of men trying to avoid the fight, then as the Indian rushed the last several yards, Doc jumped rapidly to the left and tripped him as he went by. Chagrined, the man regained his feet, then looked slowly to one side as a feint and rushed at Doc again. This time Doc did not move until the man began his downward thrust with the knife. Doc made a quick dodge to the left, dropped to one knee and thrust upward rapidly, drawing blood from the man's arm. Not a deep cut, but first blood. A warning \to the tribe and Tall Elk that this was a battle of warriors. Tall Elk became enraged and when close to Doc on this pass, leaped into the air trying to impale him on the way down. Doc went to the ground under the threatening knife, then stood tall. He no longer had a knife. Tall Elk also stood. Looking down, he saw a knife buried deep into his abdomen. He fell to his knees with a surprised look on his face. He went over, face down into the loose dirt and did not again rise.

Sitting Hawk stood at the center of the men, with his arms outspread, talking loudly.

"Take your knife and walk toward your campsite. Nashawn has your gun and a horse. I will stop most of these men, but Tall Elk had friends who's blood is on fire. Go quickly my friend. You fought an honorable fight."

Doc pulled out his knife, then walked slowly from the circle as the men made room for him to pass. It had happened so fast. He was full of thought as he walked to his campsite where he found Nashawn.

'Please come with me," he pleaded.

"John," she said. Tears were streaming down her face as she looked at him one last time. Turning, she walked away from him, back toward the tribe.

CHAPTER FIFTEEN

Doc rode the first mile fast, slowed to breathe his pony and to listen for any pursuit. The horse, Sitting Hawk had given him, was smaller than Buck, maybe fourteen hands. He had a fine easy gait. Doc had begun the ride from Jackboro as a semi-novice rider, yet now he sat his horse like he was part of it. This Indian horse was excellently trained, reacting quickly to leg pressure or the touch of the reins.

Not hearing immediate pursuit, he began a gentle canter to the north, at least approximate north. It was cloudy and Doc could see the North Star only occasionally. The trip would be difficult with immense distances to cover. There were Utes ahead, probably Comanche's behind, but he had a good horse and he felt healthier than he had for a long time. The time with the Comanche's had healed his lungs some. He could take a deeper breath now than any time since Georgia.

Perhaps no whiskey and no tobacco had also helped them feel better. He was certain he would make it to Denver. 'If,' he thought, 'if only there was a way, I could have been happy with her forever.'

He heard their horses coming after him close to dawn, still were several hour before the sun would rise. His horse was fresher, he assumed, since it had not been running hard trying to catch up. He did not know how long Sitting Hawk had delayed his pursuers, but it was a bonus of time for him. Doc increased speed just enough to stay ahead, but with the ground broken into small canyons, and arroyos, he needed to ride carefully. He passed through several dry creek beds, thought about an ambush, but he had only the Colt. He would need to be close to have any chance. He had heard rifle fire and knew they were armed with long distance weapons. One advantage he did have, they were now into Ute territory. Too much noise or action would result in an unpleasant meeting with a Ute hunting party and they would all be little but fast drying hair on a Ute lance.

Doc worked the little horse in and out of the brush always trying to head north. He was running into scrub willows mixed with a lot of mesquite and sage. Now and then, he saw cottonwoods or oak trees. He made his trail as difficult to follow as reasonably possible with the sun just lifting over the edge of the earth. But now with full light, he'd had enough. No more pursuit by Comanche's, now it was time for the hunters to become the hunted, before they woke the sleeping monster of the Utes.

He rode through a dry river wash, headed up stream through first growth willow shoots, saw a small copse of live oak ahead, and passing through them, brought his horse up the rear side of the wash, and back a hundred yards. Here, he tied the tired pony to a tree. Walking back through to the edge of the wash, he lay face down, waiting. His Colt cocked in his right hand, knife held loosely in the left, he was ready. He knew the danger of attacking the fierce

Comanche's, but he also knew he could not evade them for five hundred miles.

He heard a rock kicked by a horse fifty yards downstream. "Good, he thought, "They are tracking me." Now he knew their path and he was sure he had a solid position. His other advantage was that the superiority of numbers in any battle can lead to overconfidence and carelessness.

There were three of them, all eyes intent on his tracks. One carried a rifle, the other two carried long lances, the Comanche's traditional weapon. Doc saw that the two carrying lances also had rifles on their mounts, but still in the rifle scabbard.

At ten feet, Doc shot the rear horse in its hind flank, then fired rapidly on the other two horses. The first horse he hit swung to the left, and regained it's balance. The horses were screaming in pain and all three whirled to flee. The men were thrown from their backs. Doc ran to his pony, chased by rifle fire, leaped to the back of his animal, rode as fast as the tired beast could move for better than an hour. He could feel the energy drain from his horse and slowed it to a walk. He could hear no sounds of pursuit. This was his last gift to Sitting Hawk, he did not kill any of his pursuers. They were valuable members of Sitting Hawk's tribe. Still, both he and the horse needed water and rest. He dismounted and began walking through the night. Still watching the skies to pick up the Dipper when it showed through the clouds, the walking kept his senses alert. He stretched out the tired muscles in his legs and back. The coolness of the evening and walking unburdened would help revive his horse. He hobbled the animal and slept late in the night.

Early, Doc rode north again, after he'd rested several hours. He was able to cover ground rapidly out on the wild prairie. He still watched for the Comanche. Determined men can run down a man on a horse. The speed with which he covered ground now that he no longer had the cavalry men with him was a joy. There seemed to be unlimited vision out here, but that could be deceiving with small undulations in the land and unseen gulches where enemies could be hiding for an ambush. Still he held to a straight fast course. He relied on his eyesight. If he hadn't seen any movement, he trusted, that no one had seen him. Doc felt the strain of the long ride throughout his body, stiff painful legs and back. His head felt like it was sitting on a live nerve that sparked with every step.

The land broke up into small hills with washes and arroyos late that afternoon. Doc rounded a small butte, and saw the burned out ruin of a cabin by a small running stream. The tale of dreams and despair was written clearly in the grisly spectacle at the small ranch site, as it had been in many similar sites across the early west. This was the place where one man's hopes had died along with him.

What was left of the burned house showed a solid effort with a three room cabin with a good stone foundation. A corral had been half torn down and pieces of it had been driven deep into the yard and the man fastened to them. The dried body of the rancher had been stretched out to slowly die in the desert sun. They had staked him out with a full view of the stream for added torment. He'd been scalped and left as a warning for others. This is Indian land, stay out if you value your life.

Doc circled the homestead site. Checking for and finding no current tracks, Doc set up camp, ten rods, downstream from the burnt-out cabin. The flow of water in the small run was shallow, but fresh and cool. The horse was hobbled and spent the evening resting and feeding, while Doc ate the last of the deer he had shot the evening before.

For the best part of the remainder of the trip, as Doc remembered it, the wind was a constant. It blew hard or soft, never did it stop. He would ride through a small creek, let the horse drink, drink himself, fill the water bags and begin riding north again. The wind swirled the heat against him and within three hours, he would be incredibly thirsty again. He found a small spring one evening and camped by it, letting his animal forage and drink freely. In the morning, he drank all he could, laid down in the water to wet his clothes, but within an hour, the wind had dried his clothes, blown sand and dirt into his mouth, nose, and eyes. It seemed to have shrunken his skin until nothing on his body felt right. His skin was tender from the sand and dirt blown against his face and under his clothes. The constant abrading left him on edge. The smallest thing irritated him. He lived on venison and rabbit, both of which grew in abundance here with the lush grass. He had seen Indians on the horizon several times, but they had not approached him. He was so raw-edged by the wind that he would have encouraged a fight just to relieve his tension. Not even the sight of Alapine Springs when he rode over a hill and saw it, significantly improved his state of mind.

CHAPTER SIXTEEN

The heat had been so overpowering that day, Doc first thought the town was heat shimmers rising in a valley. When he determined that it was truly a town, he saw nothing moving but a yellow mongrel dog who sniffed and walked the main street looking for scraps of food perhaps thrown from passing horsemen or travelers. He rode to the closest bar, slid off the hot back of his horse, led it to the water trough outside the bar.

When he walked into the Dogs Leg saloon, it had been way too long since he had any whiskey. The desert and the wind had squeezed the moisture from him and the last whiskey he could recall was on the night before Macallan shot him in the back. Seemed like the fellers at the bar could have recognized a guy who needed a drink that badly and just given him a little room to indulge. But no, they were all bunched up so Doc had to push his way through them to order up a drink. The bartender wasn't very quick, so Doc shouted at him and began to bang the bar with his hat trying to get his attention.

The cowboys that Holliday had pushed through were getting a little prickly. He could feel a bristling attitude toward him. The bartender continued to ignore him, so Doc began to bang even louder on the bar with his hat. Some sand and dust turned loose from his hat and flew about the bar. Most of the men there were unappreciative of the sand and dirt from Doc's hat being in their drinks. The wrangler next to Doc was exceedingly unhappy with him. His mood did not seem to improve any when Doc pointed out to the cowboy that if he would, "Get that lazy assed bartender down here and we can both buy a glass of whiskey without the sand."

The cowboy said something negative about Holliday's parentage and drew his arm back to throw a punch. Doc pushed his hat into the man's face. While he was struggling to get his face out of the hat, Doc's boot hit him right where his front side meets the saddle and the cowboy went down hard clutching his tender parts.

Doc didn't remember much of what happened next, except that he knew there was a flurry of activity, a lot of pain, and he never did get close to a glass of whiskey.

The jail at Alapine Springs was a large frame and adobe structure. Inside, it had two containment cells on one side and a large pot belly stove and a desk with several chairs on the other. A rifle case was attached to the wall behind the desk with slots for ten rifles. Only two were in it now, seemed the plans for the rifle case were in keeping with most of the town.

The lawman, Sheriff Jakes, banged around the desk and stove long enough to wake Doc. He'd been sleeping on a loose framed mattress in one corner of a cell. There was no real bed. Holliday was hurting everywhere, but finally opened his eyes and tried to sit up. Slowly, gingerly, he stood, checking his moveable parts making sure everything was still there and still working.

"Nice to see you up," the Sheriff said. He had come in late that morning and just now was drinking his first coffee. Being Sheriff in this lightly populated county paid little but he did little real work. Now he was looking askance at his first prisoner in months. The ranch foremen usually rode in with the cowboys and for the greatest part kept them under control.

"Damn, I sure got the worst of it yesterday."

"Ya, them Double Bar J boys only get to town once a week and they can be a feisty bunch. A bad lot to pick a fight with when you are alone. Want something to eat?"

"Please, and a cup of that coffee would be greatly appreciated."

He brought Doc a plate of beans mixed with unidentifiable chunks of cold meat. There was not too much appeal to the plate.

"Come on out here and eat with me," said the Sheriff. Holliday stood, pushed the unlocked cell door open, and walked in to sit across the desk from the Sheriff. He dived into the meal. Famished, he cleaned it all up with a crust of bread and sat back with the coffee the Sheriff had poured for him.

"How'd you like it?"

"Generally speaking, I like my goat on the hoof and beef on my plate, but I was hungry enough not to care today."

"I am going to have to fine you twenty dollars for disturbing the peace yesterday."

"Damn Sheriff. You seem like a reasonable guy, twenty does seem like a lot when you know I'm broke."

"What's your name?"

"Holliday, Dr. John Holliday."

"Well Dr. Holliday, I got a headache, a toothache, and a girlfriend who is angry at me, so your troubles and woes are way down the list of my worries."

"Could be that I can help you. I am a dentist. I will pull your tooth for you if you get me a bottle of good whiskey and a small gripper over at the store. The only other cost is you waive my fine."

"You really know how to pull a tooth?"

"I'm a dentist and you got a gun. Given the situation, I'd be a fool to lie to you. I promise, take care of the whiskey and fine part, I will take care of the tooth part. You know if you take care of that bad tooth, you might treat your girl better and I will have solved all your problems. One more question though, Sheriff, where's my horse?"

"Your horse is up at the livery. Here's a ten, get a bottle of whiskey at the Dogs Leg, the tools you need from the general store and be back here as soon as you can. "

"You gonna let me just walk out of here?"

Sheriff Jakes took another drink of coffee, gently set his cup down, said, "I still have this toothache in fifteen minutes, I'm going to search you out and kill you where you stand. Got that? Timer's going. Fifteen minutes."

CHAPTER SEVENTEEN

Twenty minutes later, Doc walked back over to the Dogs Leg. Sheriff Jakes had his tooth in his hand and Doc had finished drinking the bottle of whiskey. He was short on money and patience. At least he had some whiskey in him and was in a better mood than he had been the last time he was there. He knew the owner might be a touched riled at him but he'd always been one to push his luck.

It was early and there was no one else was in the joint. He sauntered to the bar, waited for the bartender to come over. He recognized Doc immediately. "No trouble today, you hearing me?"

"No trouble from me. You the owner of this fine establishment?"

"I am and I don't need none of what you're selling, thank you very much anyway."

"You don't need none?" Doc said with a surprised look on his face. "Maybe you oughta listen to me before you make up your mind."

"You want to buy a drink?"

"Can't, I'm just out of jail and broke. I want to hire on as your faro dealer. Where you concealing your faro table and why ain't there no poker games going? Every bar west of St. Louie that can handle more than six customers has a faro table. Take a bar this size, you probably losing hundred fifty to three hundred a week in cash money."

"From all this palaver, I'm suspecting you a dealer."

"Not just a dealer, The Dealer. I'm the best in the West. I can run your faro table, host a poker table, provide your security, and guarantee you a hundred a week once we get our feet going."

You g'd awful small for such a big noise," the owner said turning toward the door to see if anyone was coming in.

"Mister," said Doc with a low steady voice which clearly spoke his intent if the bar owner had been listening carefully, "you can say yes or no to my proposition, either is your option. You make another extra comment on my size or abilities and I'm going to be forced to give you one of my special colt .45 adjustments. You might call me just a trifle touchy about my size."

Unimpressed, the man turned to Doc with a sneer on his face, "Really, you all that bad are...?"

His sentence remained unfinished as Doc grabbed the man's hair with his left hand and smashed the bar owner's face down onto the bar. As his head bounced back up, Doc's Colt smashed into the left side of his head hard enough to throw the man three feet to his left. Doc actually saw the man's boots before the large body of the bloody unconscious bartender crashed to the floor and remained silent.

Doc lifted the trap door in the bar, and went through to stand over the man behind the bar. He grabbed his hair and belt, lifted and threw him half way up on the bar.

"What's your name?" asked Doc.

"Dandy Jack," he croaked out.

"Well, Dandy Jack, you had a rough time here considering my very generous proposal to you. Made up your mind yet, or do you think you might need another little adjustment?"

"I have considered your proposal and it sounds good to me."

"Okay," said Doc. "You seem to be getting some sense now." Doc picked up a pencil and paper from near the cash register. "I'm borrowing a hundred dollars. You can take it from my first week's pay. That okay with you?"

"Yep."

"Then get off the bar, get me a bottle of whiskey, and the money. You got a faro board or do I have to build one?"

"Got one in back. Just never put it out."

"It's going up tonight. You could have done worse than getting me as your gambling partner, Dandy. I am going to make you rich."

"I don't care about rich, just leave me alive."

"One more thing along that line, Dandy, I ain't booking no blab to the Sheriff. You have a complaint, bring it to me. You probably figured out by now you should talk with a little more respect when addressing your partner. You've already seen I'm a fair man. No more adjustments unless you really need them. You double cross me you sniveling coyote and your corpse will be rotting that very night."

Doc moved into the hotel and ate at the small restaurant next door to the bar. He knew the Sheriff had taken his horse to the livery. He walked down after his evening meal to settle the bill and see if the animal was being treated nicely. He saw Buck was stabled near his pony. He asked the livery man who owned the buckskin and was told, "George English."

Doc replied, "No he doesn't. That's my horse. Put him on my bill from here on out. If you find a buyer for my other pony, sell him."

Doc walked back to the Sheriff's office. "I want to report a horse thief. That buckskin up at the livery was stolen from me out in the Indian territory. I was left afoot. If you wire Sheriff Jensen or the livery in Jackboro, Texas, they can verify that I purchased him there less than three months ago. Just between you and me, Jakes, I think a horse thief that would leave a man afoot in Indian territory ought to be hung."

"I am going to check it out, but should tell you I know George English. He owns half of the General Store here in town. He has always been law-abiding. Plus, I don't have jurisdiction out in the Indian Territory."

"He ain't in the territory now. I want my horse, pack horse, and gear including my rifle from that horse thief."

"I will check out your story and get back to you as soon as I can. In the mean time, stay away from him. I will handle it."

"Did anyone else ride in with Mr. English?"

"Seems to me it was three of them together. Mr. Mease, and Mr. Macallan rode in with him. I don't think there was anyone else. They sold a string of horses and bought into The Saloon. English works down at the General Store."

"Thanks Sheriff, glad to know all my friends made it."

CHAPTER EIGHTEEN

Dandy Jack began the gambling partnership with a white flame of hate. He recognized that there was nothing he could do right now but he kept a sawed-off behind the bar, for the first day or two, if Doc had run into trouble or been unguarded, Dandy would have cut him in half with the hawg leg.

Still, time began to work its subtle magic as his face and nose began to heal. He still presented a purple orange appearance which he explained saying, "I got thrown off that flat-headed cayuse of mine when he shied from a rattler." He noticed a distinct increase in business by the end of the third day. Doc ran the faro from three in the afternoon until eight at night. His poker game usually ran until two or three in the morning. A continual heavy tobacco fog hung in the atmosphere of greed and want exhibited by the increased number of customers now using his bar. His profit margin had significantly increased.

At the end of the week, Doc and Dandy Jack had their first powwow. "You happy with what I'm doing?" asked Doc.

"Hell, yes. You been great, wish you'd have shown up last year. Saturday night was the best night I ever had here. I'm already starting to make up another batch of whiskey."

"I like it here. Think we're doing great. The games are getting better. More people coming into play everyday. Faro's solid, been paying out pretty good, but the winners have been spending more at the bar or losing it at poker. You pour a good shot for the money. This bar is rapidly getting a name. If I was to make any suggestions to you, Dandy Jack, I think you ought to fill the shot glasses all the way to the top. If a little spills, them cowboys think it's a real bargain.

"By next year, we'll close that pile of stink, down the street. I understand it's run by Macallan and Mease. We should plan on building an out-back or buying that restaurant next door and expand the area we got. Just need to knock out a wall or two. Just things for you to think on. You still the sole legal owner, but you make me a real partner, five years from now we'll be sitting pretty.

"You sound like you want to make us rich, Doc. If you want to be my partner, I'll accept. But let's do it legal. I'll have Lawyer Hubbard draw up the papers. One thing; I want a payment of a thousand dollars, over the next year. Does that sound fair to you?" Dandy had bought the bar for five hundred dollars two years before and just been scratching out enough of a living to stay ahead in food and whiskey. "It does, Dandy," said Doc. " You get those papers and you got a partner. Tell me about George English."

"He rode into town with two other men, Lynn Mease, and Irish Macallan. They been here about three months and they already are getting to be big men in this little town. Mease and Macallan offered to buy into my bar, but I turned them down flat. They bought out the owner of the other bar, and have now changed the name to Double M. No one has seen the previous owner since they bought it, but they have the paper so it must be legal right? English began working at the general store, and now is part owner of it. I personally don't like or trust any of them."

"I'm thinking we on the same page, Dandy. In fact, I'm going down to stir things up a little."

Few things happened in his life that surprised him. Sitting Hawk's friendship had been one, but he had been mistrustful of the three cavalry men from the start. By not listening to his instincts, he had almost paid the ultimate price. He trusted what Sitting Hawk had told him, he knew that he had been betrayed by this trio. Now they would have to answer for their treachery. Three trained Cavalry men were a force each unto himself, but united their strength increased. Especially now that they were embedded into the community which provided them with 'respectability.' They would have both eyes and ears giving them information of Doc daily. They also might have additional guns on their side.

Macallan had a quick tongue and ready smile but it was only a façade covering an intelligence that was as sly and insidious as a snake. His word was given freely but was as empty of meaning as Macallan was of any honor. Doc knew he was the back-shooter. Of the three, Doc would most enjoy destroying and then killing him.

Mease was an unknown factor. His skill with weapons and his intelligence were unknown. Since he had been in the Army cavalry, he would have received some training with weapons. Without better knowledge of him, Doc rated him the most dangerous of the three.   Given that Doc had done the surgeries on him   that had saved his life, his ingratitude demonstrated a treacherous nature. He would have to be watched.

English had been the most trustworthy prior to the ambush, now he had proven himself as greedy and vicious as his partners. His skill with weapons was again an unknown but Doc believed it to be average. There was no possibility that English would face him head on or be able to beat him in a straight on encounter. Three against one was long odds, however Doc had no trouble facing long odds. Life for him was, at best, tenuous. His life was never going to be long. He believed himself to be the best of them in gun play. He had thought long and hard over his actions in provoking the three to attack him. He would need the town to push these cowards into an attack. Twice already he had been forced to leave a town. He had fought fair fights against armed opponents and still had to flee because the authorities or populous had been against him. This time he wanted to make sure he was not run out of town before all three were dead.

The sun was up before Doc. Long nights at the poker table made for late morning risings. He sat in full view at the restaurant so people could see and talk to him. He spent time in friendly talk with the citizens of the town, other late risers who were still lingering over there last cup of coffee and a smoke before starting work.

Doc wore his gun this morning. Leaving the restaurant, he walked slowly up to and entered the General Store. George English was behind the counter. There were six or seven men grouped in the store, talking to George or deciding what their purchase would be Holliday walked in. Holliday thought English looked out of place behind the counter which was piled high with bright colored candies on one side and sweet smelling jams and preserves on the other. While George was busy wrapping up a bolt of fabric a customer's purchased for his wife when he saw Holliday and was caught off guard. He turned to the customer and said, "Your Missus will love the pattern on that cloth. You're going to be happy you bought it for her. Want to put it on your account?" The man nodded, George made a notation in a book and handed the package to him. English had heard there was a new gambler/faro dealer in town, but hadn't thought it could be Holliday. He had a hard time believing anyone could survive the rifle shot from Macallan. Now Holliday was here. English's inner shame at not protecting Holliday better and not spending the time to even search for his body to see if he was still alive flushed across him, then passed quickly. This man was now their enemy who would never forgive despite English's inability to change what had happened. English's trail was headed downhill with Mease and Macallan. No changing mounts at this late date.

English struck a match and held it up in his cupped hands while he lit his cigarette and regrouped his thoughts. He decided his safest course was to brazen it out. "Holliday, how did you ever live through that ambush? Figured you was dead for sure back there. I want to tell you that we were friends on the trail and I am grateful for your help. I felt real bad when I thought you were killed back there at the Columbia."

"Happy to see me again are you, English?"

"Yes, I owe you a debt for your help on the trail."

"Sure wish you had wanted to return that help back on the Columbia when I needed it. How long did you spend searching for my body before you took my horse and gear?"

"None at all. You got shot and floated down the river." The man watched Holliday with covert hostility. "The truth is last time I saw you, you were face down in water. I thought you's dead."

"So you three assumed I was dead. Y'all figured, being dead, I wouldn't use my horse or gear, so you might just as well take them, leaving me afoot without food five hundred miles from civilization."

There was a murmur going through the men in the store. Clearly they believed abandoning a wounded companion in hostile territory to be the act of a coward.

"Any of you men want to say something?" snapped English. "Just step right up here, square your bill and then speak your piece. Probably ought to remember where you're getting credit to feed your families right now. Well come on, speak right up."

The men backed away and were silent. Several left the store, clearly they owed what was for them significant money to English.

"As for you, Holliday, you were bad shot, we thought you dead. If we had left the horse or your gear the Indians would have taken them. We had every right to take that stuff."

"I have already taken my horse back. You ride him again, I'll shoot you off his back for a thief. I want my gear back also."

"Take the horse. He's yours. As for your gear, I don't care what you want. That gear is mine. I will keep it."

"You own a gun. Sooner or later you will have to use it if you continue to follow this path."

English looked at his gun under the counter, and quickly looked away.

"Oh, I see you weighing your chances, Huckleberry. You could be a hero here in front of these people. Perhaps it would be easier if I just turned my back. You cowards always were better as back-shooters."

"You know I'm no gun fighter. I have no quarrel with you. It was only a misunderstanding."

"What I don't understand here, and am hoping you can tell me, English," said Doc, "Is what happened to you? I knew you on the trail. You were a stand up man. You were both brave and capable. I have a hard time believing you would cotton to a back-shooting. How did they get you to sell your pride?"

"Truth is, you didn't know me like you thought you did," said English.

"That misunderstanding almost cost me my life, little George English. Now I see you for what you are. Your friends won't be able to help you. They are false security. I can walk through them anytime I want. You are too big a coward to face me alone. Your best chance as I see it is to run. You better run fast George. I have an extremely low tolerance to low life's such as yourself. If you remain in town, I will be forced to rid the world of another coward. Run little George, run fast and perhaps you will be lucky and live."

The General Store customers were grouped around the two men.

"Any of you men have markers here with English and would like to pay them off, come to see me at Dogs Leg. I will help you out with much better interest. I think the town should be freed from the grip of this greedy little bloodsucker," said Doc.

"I'm Otis, from just south of town. Are you serious? Will you help us out? I have a wife and two kids to feed but I can't get ahead with the interest he charges here."

"Unlike English, I am a man of my word. See you up at the bar." Excitement such as this was rare in Alapine Springs. Talk like this frequently ended in gunfire and death. None of the men liked English, but with him holding their pledges, they could not buck him.

George knew there was no answer or action he could take that would redeem his status in the eyes of the men. "Life will be short for you here, Holliday. Take your own advice and leave."

Doc said, "I am wearing my weapon now, if you want to catch me right now. I'm thinking a coward like you will need help, but I am here if you want me. Tomorrow, I may go varmint hunting. I think there may be several skunks around. You might tell that to your partners."

CHAPTER NINETEEN

The next afternoon, Otis came up to the Dogs Leg to see Doc. He walked in quietly with his hat held in both hands. Doc looked at him quietly with his worn but clean clothes. He was middle age with a barrel chest and arms that looked strong enough to crush stone.

"Sir," he said to Doc, "I'm Otis. We talked yesterday at the General Store. You said to come here to see you if I wanted a loan to pay off my balance at the store."

Doc walked out from behind the bar, pulled a couple of chairs out from a empty table and motioned to the chair with one hand.

"I'm proud to meet you, Otis. You are the first customer of the General Store to visit me and go against English. Sit, sit for a minute and talk to me," said Doc. "You working now?"

"Oh sure, gotta a good job as a yardman out to the Double Bar J. Make thirty a month. Been working out there for old man Stuber last six years. He's always treated me good. Plus, I got my own place just south of town. It's not too big, maybe seven acres, but it's big enough for me and the missus. My wife does a pretty big garden and gets the kids to help. Got two dairy cows and a sow who just dropped a litter. There's a small barn and a few outbuildings. Really, everything we wanted."

"I'm thinking I need a man who can handle mules. Think you can handle a set of mules?"

"Certainly I can. Mules is a breeze to work with if you treat 'em right. Out to the Bar J, I do a little bit of everything and I knows mules pretty good."

"Well, here's what I'm thinking," said Doc. "I want to run a wagon from here to Pueblo, weekly. It would pick up orders from the people here in Alapine Springs, buy the goods in Pueblo, then come back and distribute them. It's thirty miles to Pueblo, so you should be able to run that and back in one day with two good mules and a stout wagon. The rest of the time, you could stay at your place and distribute the goods with your wife. Or, you could go back out to the Double Bar J and work there. Long as you get everything distributed, your time would be free. I would pay you forty a month. Ten, I would keep back until you get your loan paid off. Once you get everything paid up, you could buy the mules and wagon and run the business yourself. Do you like my proposition?"

"I like my job out at the Double Bar J. Just don't know, better talk to my wife first. What you're saying sounds good for the town though. One thing you gotta know, I ain't no fighter. I got kids I want to see grow tall. If you want a gun hand, I ain't your guy."

"I'm looking for a muleskinner, not a brawler. If fighting starts and you're there, leave, no help needed. Now, how much you owe?"

"Seventy-four dollars."

Doc gave him four double eagles. "Bring me the change and your answer tomorrow."

DOC HOLLIDAY: THE HARD RIDE

Four days later the first supply wagon rolled in from Pueblo and George England felt the economic pressure immediately.

CHAPTER TWENTY

Macallan was behind the bar on a high stool and Mease was sitting at one of the poker tables with their two hired men, Slats Calahan and Emitt Grander, when English came in to tell them Holliday was in town and looking for them.

The plan as the three saw it now was that soon, English would be the sole owner of the General Store. Another buy-out was planned. English's partner was stubborn. He absolutely refused to sell, but Macallan had decided it was time to teach him how to play poker, Macallan style.

They'd hired Calahan and Grander for their ability with both fists and guns. The new Double M was bringing in good money and a busy bar is often awash in violence. As for Holliday, Mease was all for bracing him right away. Five against one, they would easily be able to put Holliday underground. Sheriff Jakes was a joke as a lawman good for little but locking up drunks. He would not interfere in the death of Holliday. Whatever way he was killed.

"We'd be foolish to rush a fight with him now. We still hold all the cards.

Long as we have the upper hand, let's load up the odds in our favor," said Macallan.

"What'cha thinking?" asked Mease.

DOC HOLLIDAY: THE HARD RIDE

"Heard about a gunfighter operating out of Pueblo, maybe the fastest man alive, goes by the handle of Buck Brusse. We get someone with his skill, we can't lose. He will be the man that Holliday goes after first in a gunfight, giving us additional time to get a shot off at him. With five shooters and one target, we will put him down. F'r Christ sake, Brusse may get him himself. So we still would have the victory. Holliday will be dead and the blame will be put on Brusse. For five or six hundred dollars, we can have the situation totally under control. We will go back to owning this town. Damn hard to see how we don't win."

"It would take at least a week or two," said Mease.

"The fight doesn't go to the fastest, it goes to the strongest. Can't you see that with Brusse on our side, we'll easily kill Holliday, then run out anyone else that opposes us," said Macallan. "Send him a wire today. Offer an extra bonus if he makes it within the week."

"In the four months since we left the Army, we have established our future. Damn shame that bastard showed up," English said. "Soon we'll be back raking in money."

"I'm not disagreeing with you, but let's consider going to talk to him first, see what he wants. Maybe we can buy him out. The cheapest way to shake this long-necked monkey off our back might just be money. We can always use force if we need to," said Mease. "I know I could break that skinny, whiskey sucking, southerner in half any time I wanted, with guns or fists."

"Well we gotta do something soon, he's cut into our profit with the store, loaning money to my customers so they could pay their bills off. I've heard from the citizens that he is sending a weekly wagon up to Pueblo to buy cheaper stuff and bypass my store all together," said English.

I think it's time for the boys to be getting some fresh air. What day does the wagon roll?" asked Macallan.

CHAPTER TWENTY-ONE

Doc, sitting at a poker table with four other players, watched the three men stroll casually in and line up against the bar for a drink. Dandy Jack's bar was a tree, split in two, boarded together and sanded smooth. The front edge was a smaller three inch tree which had been halved and nailed into place. The surface of the bar was stained with spilled whiskey, burned with misplaced cigarettes and carved by idle men with knives.

Mease and English each had one leg up on the foot rail. They turned with glasses of whiskey held tightly in gloved hands and looked at Doc, still sitting at the table. Holliday threw in the hand he was playing.

"Be back in a few minutes, gentlemen," he said to the four men sitting at his table.

"Looks like old friends have come to visit."

Then to the men at the bar, he said, "I am so relieved to see the three of you made it. I thought you all died in an ambush back on the Columbia. Instead, seems like maybe there was only a bushwacker. He shot me in the back and left you all unharmed. Shame none of you felt the need to help me, but I suppose you were busy running."

"We were a little busy trying to stay alive. I understand you're disappointed in us, but we thought you to be dead. You were floating face down in the river, not moving at all, while we were fighting for our lives. The Indians were on us before we could help you. We barely got out of that spot alive. Still, we feel bad and would like to pay for the gear you lost. Also, we'd like to discuss a little business with you," said Macallan.

Holliday walked up and joined them at the bar. He was wary of them but felt they would not openly attack him with witnesses here in the bar. Dandy Jack standing by his scatter gun behind the bar looked to be paying no attention, be he was a further deterrent. He had moved to the place on the bar where he could easily cover all three.

"What kind of business you want to discuss with me?"

"Mease and I purchased the Double M saloon up the street and have been doing pretty good. George owns half the General Store, his business is advancing also. We know you're just starting here, so we would like to purchase your interest here in the Dogs Leg. We'd pay a fair price and give you an extra two hundred dollars for your gear and traveling money. We feel this would be a way to compensate you for any trouble we might have caused you."

"Wow, Dandy Jack, did you hear that? These gentlemen want to go into business with you. Whatcha think? You want to be in business with them?"

Dandy pulled his shotgun out from under the bar and laid it in plain view.

" My bar is stained and rough but I find I am fond of it and cannot sell. Also, I have this," nodding his head at the gun, "And while I have it, they will not have the bar."

"Well Gentlemen, there is your answer. Perhaps my partner could have been more gracious in his response, but I believe you understand his answer fully. He don't want no business with you. As for myself, I plan on killing the man who shot me in the back before I leave town. I'm find that I am not so foolish as to believe we were attacked by Indians. From what I've seen, none would not have survived an Indian ambush. I believe one of you brave little Cavalrymen shot me in the back. Mease was too sick, English still had backbone, so Macallan's the one. If you other two brave men want to back away from him, I can just kill him here, right now, and save us all a bunch of time. What sayest thou Mac, are you the brave back shooter?"

Holliday's response to their offer and his demeaning insulting way of talking to them had irritated Mease from the second they had walked in the door. He regretted now that he had suggested buying Doc out and he knew only a direct confrontation would move Holliday. Doc was walking past the three men, who were still leaning on the bar. His attention was mostly on Macallan, waiting for his response to his accusation. Doc knew better than to ignore Mease or George as all three were treacherous. Stopping, Holliday faced his enemy and stood ready to respond to any action taken by Macallan. Mease's right hand had been lying casually on his gun belt until Doc stopped before them at the bar. Mease's fist suddenly flew up at Doc's face with one hundred and ninety pounds of solid muscle behind the blow.

Holliday's dodging response to the blow was so fast that the punch slipped passed him completely.   Mease had committed himself totally to the assault and was thrown off balance to the right. He turned his head trying to see what Doc was doing, as he struggled to right himself.   The hard gray steel of Doc's gun smashed into his face, before he was aware Holliday was swinging it. Mease fell to the bar floor hard and landed flat on the base of his spine. Before he could rise, Doc fired a .45 caliber round into the floor less than four inches from Mease's head. Doc then pulled his knife and held it at the stunned man's throat.   "You miserable sneaky son of a pig, you came into my saloon to attack me. Clearly the alley slime that fathered you never bothered teaching you manners. Well, I can. Do not move your head or I will leave it laying around on my floor for the next year or two. Now would not be a good time for you to develop courage, Mr. Mease. You probably should lay there quietly like the coward you are. Were you the one who back shot me?"

"No, it wasn't me." Mease lay still. Finally Doc pulled his knife back from the downed man's throat and moved back. English and Macallan helped Mease to his feet.

"Did you hear that, Macallan?" said Doc. "Mease just admitted I was shot in the back, although he claims he was not the shooter. That leaves just you and English to pay for the treachery."

As the three left the bar, Mease shouted, "I'm going to get you Holliday, I'm going to get you!" Doc walked to the doors, swung them open and stepped through. He faced the three men standing in the street less that fifteen feet from him.

"I'm right here. Feel like you want to get me now?" said Doc.

The three men continued to back away. Doc continued to watch them, "Sometimes, you gotta just spin that wheel. Feel like luck could be with you today?"

"The time is coming," said Macallan.

"I will be right here waiting for you, Daisy Boy. Try to work up the courage to face me and stroll on back."

Early the next morning, Otis knocked at Doc's hotel door.

CHAPTER TWENTY-TWO

"They's on me before I could do anything. They caught me about fifteen miles out where the creek cuts through by that sharp bend in the road. There was no outrunning them. One whacked me unconscious with a rifle butt. When I come to, the wagon was burning. All I could do to get d'em mules unhitched and they skittered off quick. No chance to catch them. D'em idjits had masks over their faces, but any fool could easily see it was Calahan and Grander from up at the Double M saloon. Grander's the one as hit me. That bastard is lower than the track of a rattlesnake's belly. Took most of the day and half the night for me to walk back in."

"I'll take care of this," said Doc. "Damn sorry you got hurt. Just take the next couple days off and then I'll be down to see you. And Otis, forget the money you owe, I'm just wiping that off. I figure to get that much out of the hides of those two sons a bitches."

"Sorry I couldn't do more to protect the wagon, but I ain't no fighter."

"I hired you as a muleskinner, not a fighter, Otis. I'll take care of the fighting part. You did exactly right."

"I's coming down to quit, Doc. Goona tell you to find someone new. All the way into town I was thinking 'bout what I could tell you when I quit. When I got home, they'd roughed up my wife some. Scared her and the kids bad. They burned my barn. Lucky my little guy got the cows out safe. But they shot my sow and half of her litter. Just plain meanness. Never had any call to mix in my family."

"I'm sorry they did that Otis. I will make them pay."

"You don't understand, Doc. I ain't no fighter, that's true. But now, when you go to get them, you can count me in. Ain't no one ever oughta raise a hand to my wife or scare my kids. I will shoot them weasels down in a heartbeat. And I ain't quitting. Those egg-sucking dogs ain't chasing me off."

"Thanks for your support, Otis. If I need help, I will look for you."

Doc sat outside the Dogs Leg on one of the chairs he took from a poker table. He opened the stogie that Dandy Jack had given him a while back. He bit the end off, lit a match and ran the flame up and down the side of the cigar to warm it. With the second match he lit it, checked the lit end to make sure it was all burning and settled back, watching the Café. He puffed slowly. It went out several times and he had to relight it. An observer would believe Doc was thoroughly absorbed in and enjoying his smoke.

Slats Calahan and Emitt Grander walked up the sidewalk, looked at Doc once, then entered the Café and took seats opposite each other next to the window. Doc relit his cigar one more time, blew the smoke high, then tossed the chewed up butt, still smoking, out on the street. He stood slowly, stretched and began to walk slowly down to the Café.

Grander was seated so as to watch the door. He looked up as

Doc came slowly through the door. As the door swung shut, Doc took two quick steps, grabbed Calahan by his hair and smashed his face hard down into his plate of food. Calahan's nose split, throwing blood across the face of the table. Doc released his head go, slipped his hand forward, grabbed Calahan's coffee and threw the scalding liquid into Grander's face as he was trying to stand up. He was reaching for his gun. Both of his hands went immediately to his face to protect his eye. Doc's .38 hit him hard just above his right ear and his head flopped to the left, breaking the pane of glass next to him. Calahan had raised his head and was trying to stand as Doc's .38 continued on in its trip, hitting the man hard on the nose which had just been broken. Calahan and his chair went over backward with the force of the blow. He head smashed hard onto the floor. neither Calahan or Grander moved as Doc, standing over them, cocked his .38.

"Understand you gentlemen have been busy on the road twixt here and Pueblo. Now I want to know which one of you brave gents hit Otis's wife?"

Both men looked at him with hate in their eyes. Neither man said a word.

"Now men, just so's you understand, I'm only moderately irritated right now. You keep me standing here much longer and I'm going to be angry. You best speak up quick before I start decide to ventilating both of you. Haven't made up my mind which of you pig-eyed idiots to dispatch first."

"Stop right there, Holliday. Drop your gun, raise your hands, and step back."

"Sheriff Jakes, I will step back and let them go, but I'm not dropping my gun. Either one of these men would kill me immediately." Doc stepped back, reholstered his gun and turned to face Jakes.

"You two, Grander, Calahan, get up and get out of here. You want to press charges, come by my office later."

The two men left, looking hate at Doc.

Doc turned to the owner and said, "I'll pay all the damages."

Sheriff Jakes asked, "What was that all about?"

"They roughed up Otis's wife and burned his barn while he was out on the road. I can not abide a man who would hit a woman. They also attacked Otis out on the road, destroyed the wagon and left him unconscious. I can't let them get by with violence to one of my employees or their family. Are you going to arrest me?"

"Why? You drunk? Everyone in the county knows I'm good for nothing but locking up drunks," said Jakes. "Far as I'm concerned, you could have shot both of them and I would have bought a medal for you. It takes a special lowdown kinda skunk to hit a woman."

"Come on over to the bar and I'll buy you a drink," said Doc. The two left the restaurant together.

CHAPTER TWENTY-THREE

Kate came in on the afternoon stage. She had discovered Doc's location from the wire sent by Sheriff Jakes to determine the ownership of the buckskin horse in the livery. As Doc kissed her hand in greeting, she said, "Sorry I couldn't make it earlier, John. I had business to take care of in Denver." Doc set her up in an adjoining room at the hotel. They spent the early evening reacquainting themselves with the passion they felt for each other. They shared several glasses of whiskey and a few cigarettes. Her body was still as spectacular as he remembered.

Later, they ate at the café and Doc went to start his faro table. Kate started to work at the Dogs Leg that night. Being a prostitute was Kate's choice. It was her chosen profession, something she was good at and enjoyed. As a headstrong woman, desiring her independence above all, it was one of the few professions open to her. The addition to the bar of a beautiful working whore could only increase their business. Later that night, Doc saw blood speckles coughed into his handkerchief. The combination of late hours, little fresh air, tobacco and a diet of whiskey with little food was having a debilitating effect on his health.

Doc woke early that morning with a wracking coughing. He was slow in rising, poured a small glass of whiskey to stop the cough, then lit a small lamp before walking down the hall to relieve himself and wash his face. Less than ten feet down the hall from his room, he heard three rounds crash through the hotel window and into his sleeping space. He stopped, lit his first small cigar for the day. He waited several minutes after the firing stopped, then entered the room. His bed had been ripped open by one of the rounds. Had he still been sleeping when that bullet hit his bed, death or a serious injury would have been certain. He walked down the stairs into the street. Crossing over the street, he banged on the door to the Sheriff's office.

"Yeah, yeah, what the hell you want this early in the morning?"

"I'm making my dental rounds. How is your jaw this morning?" asked Doc.

"That was a time back. Whatcha really here for?"

"Have you any coffee made, and if you have, might I have a cup?" asked Doc.

"Help yourself."

Doc picked up an empty cup from the Sheriff's desk, filled it with coffee, then sat in the chair in front of his desk. "Oh, by the way, since I'm here anyway, I better tell you that someone is using my hotel room for target practice. Being as you are the curious type, I thought you might like to know."

"So that's what those shots were. Sounded like a Spencer to me. What do you think?"

"It was a Spencer."

"Any idea on who it was?

"Lots of ideas, no proof," said Doc.

"Well," said Sheriff Jakes, "Being as I'm the curious type, I'll go over to your room and look around. Maybe I can see something. By the way, checked out that horse, it's yours. The gear you lost is not recoverable under the law. It turns out they should have taken it to prevent it from falling into hostile hands."

"Thanks for checking, Sheriff. Appreciate your help." Doc left the office, walked back toward the hotel. The swampers were sweeping the old cigarette butts from the previous night out onto the sidewalk prior to swabbing down the floor of the saloon. His body was shaken by another severe spasm of coughing, he looked down with fatal acceptance at the blood in his handkerchief. He had Kate back with him. He had his old life back. And his tuberculosis was back. His mind was slowly coming to accept that everything he wanted in life was that which he could never have. The life he was forced to live would soon destroy him. Fate in its cruelty forced him to meet Nashawn so he would see how wonderful life could be before sending him back to exist in this hell. Perhaps his only consolation was that he would soon be moving to the Elysian Fields.

Climbing the stairs, he gave Kate a gentle nudge. "Let's go down for a drink, before breakfast, my sweet, that I may bathe my eyes in your early morning luster."

"I love the way you talk, John. You have truly wasted your life. You should have been a poet with your gentle soul."

"Only a soul as lovely and pure as you could know that, Kate, my little beauty."

Having slept little, Mease saddled his horse early and rode south of town for several miles. He circled the back bluff, climbing high into the tall pines. Riding quietly on a hundred years of fallen needles, he worked his way back to the front of the bluffs by first light. He tied his horse back thirty feet into the trees and walked to where he could see the back of the hotel. He counted the rooms, three from the left wall of the hotel. Laying on his stomach, he watched for a light to come on in the room. He aimed carefully with his Spencer and sent three rounds through the room's window when the lamp was lit.

Quickly now, he retraced his steps. Riding as rapidly as possible, he worked his way around behind the General Store and tied his horse there. Now he was across the street and a block north of Holliday, watching him walk with Kate to the Dogs Leg. Mease had drunk much the night before and had seethed all night with humiliation from the beating Doc had given him the day before. He watched Doc leave the hotel, and cursed the luck that had kept his rounds from ending the life of the little man. Doc was unsteady on his feet, as he stepped into the bar with Kate. Within minutes they came out, heading for the restaurant. Mease could see Doc was a pasty white color, his hands appeared to be trembling. Clearly his cough had returned with debilitating results. Now would be the time to buck him. Kill him or drive him from the town. There was no living with Doc being in the same town, his presence reminding them every day of their cowardly betrayal of an ally and the added insult of Doc beating him with his pistol.

Mease waited by the entrance to the saloon. He checked his gun again quickly. He was ready. Time for this southern peckerwood to bite street dust. As Doc came out of the restaurant door following Kate, for whom he had held the door, Mease sauntered slowly across the sidewalk and stood twenty feet from his enemy. Doc was still leaning on the door jamb with his left hand appearing to hold himself steady. His right hand was hanging loose by his side.

"Well, well, well," said Doc. "Kate, my dear, this poor man in front of us is Mr. Mease. He has a grudge against me. Perhaps feeling I unfairly saved his life when he was injured. It appears his courage has been enhanced by whiskey and an overblown belief in his own capabilities. He has become brave enough to come at me without his friends to back his play. Are you going to be the sunshine of the day for the weasel pack? Could you be playing the part of lion not mouse here Mr. Mousey Measey?"

Doc began walking slowly toward Mease. Mease had been certain he could defeat the sick man minutes ago, now he was standing alone looking at one of the deadliest gunfighters the west ever produced. He knew instantly how the rat feels when it sees the cobra for the first time. Doc's eyes were flat black showing no emotion. He had absolutely no fear and it showed. No hesitation. Malice flowed outward with every step.

As Mease began to back away from the confrontation, Doc kept advancing at him.

"Do you feel you may need a little whiskey to get that courage up? Or are you looking for friends to show up to help you. I believe we should play our little game out to the end here. I suppose I could just turn my back to you, I know you are braver with a back shooting."

DOC HOLLIDAY: THE HARD RIDE

Mease was aware of the people beginning to gather to watch him back leather. He was being made to look less than a man.

"Perhaps it is too early for your courage be fully grown. Or do you think your gun here has become a little too heavy to lift. I believe my lovely companion will help you lift it from your holster if you find your strength has become insufficient."

Mease's eyes searched the men on either side, trying to find an ally. No one was coming forth to help. Alone, desperate, he made the fatal error of reaching for his weapon. "God damn you to hell, Holliday." Mease's right shoulder dropped, he stepped slightly to the left, and almost cleared his holster by the time Doc's two .38 caliber rounds entered his chest. The pistol had been held behind Holliday's back in his left hand. Doc finished the execution by putting one more round into Mease's forehead. A listener may well have thought only one round was fired, so rapidly were the three missiles sent on their deadly mission.

Mease was thrown almost fifteen feet backward by the force of the blasts. His body lay lifeless while his left leg continued to jerk several times. Then he lay still.

As Doc and Kate walked past the dead man, Doc said, " It's so wonderful having you here to spend time with my dear."

The Sheriff came running with his gun drawn. Seeing Mease lifeless on the sidewalk, he holstered his gun. "Doctor Holliday, can you tell me what happened?"

"I believe I can, Sir. I think this young man became hopelessly smitten by the loveliness of my companion. He felt he should dispatch me to enhance his efforts in securing her affections. I chose not to be dispatched. Truly a case of love showing its cruel, unforgiving side. I also believe that if you ask several of the witnesses here, you will find that the former Mr. Mease drew on me. I was only protecting myself."

CHAPTER TWENTY-FOUR

Later that afternoon, Macallan, in the aftermath of death, had a striking visitor to his saloon. A tall long legged lady walked into the bar with a rustling of taffeta and swirling of skirts that brought Irish to his feet. She stood at the bar and ordered a shot of whiskey. In her early thirties with masses of blonde ringlets escaping from a flower bedecked bonnet, she was the most beautiful thing Macallan had ever seen. She clearly knew her way around a saloon.

"Can I help you, Miss?"

"Well yes, I believe you can. Are you, Macallan, the owner of this fine establishment?"

"I am," murmured Irish, surprised that she knew his name.

"Please bring me the drink I ordered, and if you wish to be a gentleman, you could buy it for me."

"Certainly, Miss. Here, sit here," he said, sweeping around the bar with a glass full of his best. He pulled out a chair, and helped her to sit. "I would be proud to buy you a drink."

Placing his own drink down on the table in front of the chair next to her, he sat, then looked up at her quickly. "My first name is Irish. You already know my last name and that I own this place. Can I ask what your name is?"

She took a long look at him, glancing casually around the bar before she answered. "I'm Sue. Friends call me Waco Sue. I hope you and I are going to be friends."

Irish drank a good swirl of red-eye, swallowed hard, then cleared his throat before he looked back at her. "I would like to be your friend. Where are you from Sue?" Always friendly with women before he came to the West, now he found himself almost shy before this stunning blonde lady.

"My skunk husband abandoned me in Denver. Best thing that piebald mangy dog ever did for me. I moved down here because I like a smaller town. More opportunity in a small town."

Irish, slow in understanding, finally came around to what she was saying. "You looking for a job here in the bar?"

"Oh hell, you quick with a gun as you are on the uptake? I got two girls with me. The girls names are Fat Gerty and Sally Mae. They are both experienced whores. They will make as little trouble for you as possible, but you gotta understand, girls and drunks can end up in fights. We will live upstairs and work the bar for drinks between dates. No specials for the staff you have here." She lifted her drink to Irish. "Here's to a successful business venture."

Macallan lifted his drink, feasted his eyes on her, then asked, "Would you like to shake hands to seal the deal?"

"Sounds good to me," said Sue. "Maybe we could go up those stairs there and find a more friendly way to close this deal." She smiled her sly smirky little smile.

By the time Waco Sue, and her girls, began to work that evening, Irish was well smitten by Sue's smile, the enchanting way she walked, and the strong spirit of freedom she lived by. Best of all was that she knew her way around a bedroom. He would not soon forget the wild afternoon of Sue.

Sue had left Fort Richardson four months earlier. Her new husband, 'The Colonel' had been ordered back East for a new assignment. Two months later they were in Denver. A week after that, she woke up alone. He had deserted the Army, stolen his companies payroll, skipped out on her, sold everything she had that he could raise money on, and vanished. She had been suspicious when he courted her and asked her to marry him. She couldn't resist his charm and was soon married.

It wasn't like she was a fine parlor lady. She was accepting of anyone with the price. Still the respectable, handsome man with a dashing spirit courting her and wanting to be married to her had excited her. Men were a difficult, almost alien species, to understand. From Waco Sue's perspective, most of their decisions seemed to be made based upon the amount of frequent sex they could get. And while men always seemed to approach the prettiest whores first, by nights end the homeliest always had the same amount of business. The busiest time Fat Gerty had enjoyed, was while she was pregnant. Her earnings during the last three months she carried her child, averaged over fifty dollars more per day. In truth, it was just a woman they were wanting to use, but perhaps a pretty face inserted a small amount of imaginary romance into the encounter. Perhaps Fat Gerty's pregnancy made them feel like married men.

When the evening ended, Fat Gerty and Sally Mae had retired up the stairs and Macallan was locking up the whiskey for the evening, when Waco Sue asked, "Just where do you think you are going off to this evening, Big Guy?"

"I was heading home."

"I don't hardly think so." In a soft voice, low enough to make Macallan listen harder, Sue said, "You better just spend a little time on changing that plan. You should start working on how you can keep your business partner happy. I think you'll find life is better if you keep me happy. Come with me now, bring along a bottle of your best whiskey, and we'll talk." The next morning, Macallan went to the restaurant and brought back two heaping plates of food for his first ever breakfast in bed. He was in love, he had inserted a small amount of imaginary romance into his encounter with the lovely Sue.

CHAPTER TWENTY-FIVE

The next morning English and Macallan were both at the bar before noon. Calahan and Grander were already sitting at a table waiting for them. The damage inflicted by Holliday was very visible on their faces. Plans would have to be changed. Mease's death changed everything. George had looked to Mease because of his steady even-handed way of dealing with problems. Now, he was looking at Waco Sue, a pretty whore, two 'tough' security men who had been beaten like rented mules, and an overconfident Macallan saying 'nothing has really changed.' Everything had changed. No one in his alliance did anything to bolster his confidence.

"When is Brusse due?" asked English.

"Shit, I don't know." said Macallan. "He doesn't stay in close contact with me. I was hoping he'd be here by now."

Sue went behind the bar, set up five glasses, carefully filled each with the best whiskey they had, then walked around the bar and carrying one glass to each of the men seated at a table. She took the last glass for herself and sat with them.

"Mease was a fool," said Macallan. " He never should have braced Holliday himself. We knew he wasn't a team-player. It seems to me we had some dead weight that just unloaded itself from our wagon. Calahan and Grander may not look the prettiest after being caught off guard, but they are capable and ready fight. With Brusse to lead us, we will easily put him down. I think we have to have patience until Brusse arrives. He's fast enough to get rid of Holliday himself." Macallan raised his glass, "Now here is to the new Three, George, Irish, and my choice to replace Mease, Waco Sue. What say George? Will you accept Sue as an equal partner with you and me?"

George didn't like Waco Sue, but he knew without Macallan he had no chance to live through the coming weeks. "Certainly I accept her. Welcome Sue."

The three clinked glasses together and drank. "Yes," said Macallan, "We can do it."

The doors to the bar swung open and a tall, hawk-faced man dressed in black with his gun tied low, leather thronged down, entered the room. He looked at the three seated conspirators. "I'm Buck Brusse. Which of you sent for me?"

It had been a normal business day in the small town when Brusse had ridden in. People had been moving on the street, children were running, playing, and horses were tethered before many of the businesses. As word of Brusse's arrival blew up and down the community, the people began to disappear. Mothers were rounding up their children and the horses were all gradually moved out of harm's way.

One hour later, dead in the heat of the afternoon sun, the five men were out on the street walking toward the Dogs Leg. Brusse walked in the middle, flanked by English to his right and Macallan to his left. Macallan carried a scatter gun and a side arm.

172

Everyone else wore only his side arm. Brusse motioned for Grander to walk the north side of the street, Calahan walked up the south side. They stopped fifty feet from the bar. Macallan called Holliday out.

"We know you're in there. Come out and face us before we come in and shoot you down like the mongrel dog you are."

Inside the Dogs Leg, Doc looked out the window at the three men in the middle of the street and the two walking along the sides.

"Seems like long odds out there Dandy, you with me or not?"

"You miserable little whiskey sucking sum bitch. I'm right behind you with my bar gun. I still don't like you, but man's gotta stand up for his partner." Dandy Jack checked his loads.

"Yah, I know, grown damn fond of you too, Dandy."

Carrying the .38 stuck in his waistband, near his left hand, and his .45 in its holster, Holliday stepped out onto the sidewalk and leaned against the post holding up his sign. Dandy Jack came out and stood to his right. Shotgun already up and cocked.

Sheriff Jakes came walking out from a side street. "You men stop right where you are. You will not turn my town into a war zone."

Macallan said, "This is between us, Jakes. No sense in getting yourself killed. When it's over and done with, we'll make it square with you."

Doc said, "Thanks for the help, Jakes, but this is my job. You truly don't get paid enough to stop this. How about you just check the livery stable and come back in a few minutes." Jakes backed off to the side. Then he walked quickly from the street. Doc rested a moment, closed his eyes, felt Nashawn's lips on his one last time and stepped out into the street. Buck Brusse looked carefully at him. "Are you Doc Holliday?"

"Yes, Mr. Brusse, I am. I recognize you as well. You have enjoyed wide notoriety for your indifference to human life."

"Well just hold this up a minute. They never said nothing about facing Doc Holliday. They're wanting to pay me a measly five hundred dollars to kill you. That's way too little for Doc Holliday. I want a thousand to kill him. Up it now or I walk." said Brusse.

"You'll get a thousand," said Macallan.

"So you've stepped out of the shadows finally, Mr. Macallan. Will you admit yet that you're the one who bushwacked me?" said Doc.

"Not that it matters now, but I was the one, "said Macallan.

"Oh poor little Macallan, I suspect you wish you were back in New York this morning, instead of meeting your death here on a lonely street. In New York, you may have been special, but here you will not be finishing your day as the springtime Daisy of your little band.

Brusse removed a black leather glove from his right hip pocket and began to slowly pull it on his hand. "I've heard a lot about you, Doc. This time there will be no tricks or knives. Have you ever faced a man straight on before?"

"I seem to recollect other fools such as yourself, now that you mention it. Don't remember any one stupid enough to die for such a piddling amount before. But then I always heard you were, at best, only piddling. Please feel free to reach for your weapon any time you wish. Perhaps you will be the one to end my suffering on

174

this earth. If not, I would hate to have my afternoon lunch delayed for such a small annoyance."

Brusse shrugged his shoulders, flexed his right hand, and adjusted his stance to face directly at Doc. He slowly lowered his hand until it was slightly below his gun, which was tied to his right leg.

Doc saw Brusse's face contract, at the same time as his hand moved toward his pistol. As his gun came out of the holster, Doc whipped a bullet at the man. There was a roar and a brush of breeze passing by as Macallan fired his scatter gun, hitting nothing but the Dogs Leg behind Doc and Dandy Jack. Doc's nerves were wire taut as he saw his bullet catch Brusse's left shoulder. The gun fighter fought back against the force pulling him sideways and backwards. As Brusse pulled his body straighter, his gun was leveled at Doc again. Doc's second round caught him and he shifted visibly in the morning heat. His gun fired twice as he slowly pitched forward on his face to pour his life's force into the dust of the street. The smell of powder filled Doc's nose; his sight was reduced by the cloud of burned gunpowder surrounding him. He found himself screaming and moving with relentless fury at Macallan and English. Doc's gun, still smoking, was leveled at where the hired gun had stood.

Dandy's scattergun roared and Grander's legs were blown out from under him. He crashed loudly to the wooden sidewalk. Dandy's second barrel ripped into his chest and flung him backward in spiral turn to his right. His body lay motionless, with his legs still on the sidewalk, while his upper body lay leaking blood onto the dusty street.

A rifle shot rang out from behind Calahan. He was hit hard on his left arm, right below the shoulder. He righted himself, drew his gun with his right hand, looked back quickly to see Waco Sue holding a smoking rifle. He stepped from the street into the alley between two buildings and out of her line of fire. He refocused his eyes on Doc. He raised his pistol to aim, but felt a sharp blow to his body which knocked him back against the building. He turned his head quickly to see Otis pulling his axe back for another swing. He tried to twist and raise his gun as his face disappeared in a four foot spray of misty red. The force of Otis's blow severed the top half of his head. The lifeless body bounced off the sun-baked wood and lay motionless in the street. Waco Sue, standing a half a block behind Macallan, raised her rifle. "We're even now Kate. Thanks for killing the Colonel."

Macallan had fired both barrels of his shotgun at Doc when Brusse begun to make his play. In his haste, both loads went high, hitting neither Doc or Dandy, but ripping large pieces of wood from the front of the saloon. He glanced quickly at English, dropped the hawg leg and grabbed wildly at his side arm.Doc changed the line of his .45 caliber and squeezed off a round. It pierced Macallan's chest before Irish had time to level his gun up. His body shot backward and lay lifeless in the dirt of the street.

English threw his hands into the air, "Don't shoot. Don't shoot."

"Oh, Georgie, it's hard to see the real face of the smiling weasels you called your friends. Still, it was your trail, you chose it. You have to pay."

"I'm not going to fight you."

"Then I might just have to shoot you down where you stand, you greedy turncoat Yankee."

As Doc leveled his pistol at English, Dandy Jack grabbed him from behind, forcing his gun downward in a grip Doc could not break. Dandy held him tight saying, "Here comes Jakes."

It took several minutes for Doc to gain control of himself. As the blind fury drained from him, he said, "Looks like you're safe for now, George. You came close to dying here today. You be sure and tell your grandkids, a man named Dandy Jack, saved your life."

Sheriff Jakes walked up to the group, looking at English who was still wearing his sidearm. "Damn, this had to be some fight. Looks like you killed half my town. With the reputation Brusse had, I thought no one could beat him."

Waco Sue said, "From what Macallan told me, you might want to closely examine the deed to the bar. Your Mr. English there, together with his two dead compatriots, have been really bad boys." Sheriff Jakes turned to English, "I'll take that weapon. You are under arrest."

"What are you charging me with?'

"I ain't quite sure yet. Disturbing the peace to start with." Sheriff Jakes removed English's weapons. Then began walking him toward the jail. "Oh, you might like to know, I got a wire from the Federal Marshall out of Dodge City. He wants you held prisoner until he can get here. Something was said about Desertion."

Big Nose Kate walked over to Waco Sue. The two began to talk quietly in the shade of a building.

Doc turned to Dandy Jack. "How about that my friend, we won. Bet you'd never have guessed that. "

"I have come to believe you can do anything, Doc. And this really hurts to say, but I believe you are a good man and my friend."

"Damn, Jack, don't go around spreading any rumors about me being a good man. I am going to be leaving town, Dandy. You are going back to being the sole owner. If I was you though, I would sure talk to that crazy blonde whore about working in the Dogs Leg."

"We got a good business going here. Why leave?"

"Town's too small. I need city life."

"Going to Denver?"

"Fuck Denver, I'm heading off to Tombstone. Love the name of that town."

ABOUT THE AUTHOR

David is a former U.S. Navy Corpsman who spent time attached to the Marine Corps. He earned a Bachelor's degree from Northwestern College and Master's degree from Western Illinois University. He currently resides in Port St. Lucie, Florida, with his wife and three dogs.

WEBSITE: http://www.tienterd.com/author/
FACEBOOK: https://www.facebook.com/Dave.Tienter